An Unexpected Governess

Lelia M. Silver

Silver Summer Publishing

An Unexpected Governess

Published by Silver Summer Publishing
http://www.leliamsilver.com

The characters and events portrayed in this book are fictitious or are used fictitiously. Any similarity to real persons, living or dead, is purely coincidental and not intended by the author.

ISBN-13: 978-1-965406-02-1

DEDICATION

To Isaiah and Indya. Thank you for giving me new insight into my characters' hearts. I know your love story will have just as happy an ending as this book.

ACKNOWLEDGMENTS

This book would never have gotten this far without the support and encouragement of my husband and my dear friends and family members. My thanks also go out to all those who have taken a chance and read my works. Your support and encouraging words are more appreciated than you can know. In addition, I must acknowledge the brilliance of Jane Austen. Her characters, plots, and settings are unparalleled. Of course, any mistakes are my own.

Mary was the only daughter who remained at home; and she was necessarily drawn from the pursuit of accomplishments by Mrs. Bennet's being quite unable to sit alone. Mary was obliged to mix more with the world, but she could still moralise over every morning visit; and as she was no longer mortified by comparisons between her sisters' beauty and her own, it was suspected by her father that she submitted to the change without much reluctance.
– Pride and Prejudice

PROLOGUE

It all started with a letter. One heart-wrenching, tear-jerking, earth-shattering letter. In the space of a moment, of a sentence, everything changed. Thomas Bowen's life would never be the same.

That letter was the reason he had left his comfortable home in Hertfordshire and journeyed to Portsmouth. Now, he stood high on Portsdown Hill, overlooking the town and harbor below. The gray skies matched his dull mood and the town spread before him was dingy and repulsive in comparison to the bright fields he had traveled from. It was hardly welcoming. He hesitated to descend into the town itself, afraid of what waited for him below.

He knew in the end he would, as it was expected of him, and he could hardly forsake the responsibility that awaited him. But still he dawdled, turning his hat round and round in his hands as the skies threatened to open up on him.

He was not normally a man of inaction. His estate, Kaverstow, had flourished under his competent guidance. But he was a man used to his own company and his own comforts, without the distractions of a family.

He led a carefully ordered life. Breakfast was served precisely at 8:00 a.m., and dinner at 6:00 p.m. He spent his days either in his study with his ledgers or with his steward in the fields. In the evenings, he entertained himself with a book before a warm fire. He very rarely attended any social functions, as he found them quite tedious and taxing. His retiring nature and awkward manners were not well-suited to the ballroom or parlor.

Still, he was quite pleased with his life. It suited him just fine the way things were. It was the knowledge that all this was about to change that frightened him.

No member of his household would dare to upset his sensibly orchestrated existence. He chewed anxiously on his bottom lip. But it was not the current members of his household he was worried about. His home was about to be invaded by four small strangers, and he had no doubt that his comfortable life was about to be turned upside down.

It was sad, really, that they were strangers. He had been very fond of his younger sister before she had married a navy man and moved to Portsmouth. He had intended to visit her, of course, but somehow Kaverstow had always occupied his time, and Anne had been far too busy running her little household in her husband's absence to travel to Hertfordshire.

They had taken for granted that they had all the time in the world to close the distance that had gaped between them. He sighed. And now it was too late.

Anne was gone, and he would never have the chance to see her, settled in her home, proud of her efficiently run household, with her children gathered around her and her beloved husband nearby.

He would have preferred that his nieces and nephew had known him before now. It would make things infinitely easier. As it was, they would no more recognize him than he would them. And he had come to take them away from the only home they had ever known.

He sighed again and replaced his hat on his head as rain began to drizzle from the sky. It was a thankless task he had to do, but he had best be on with it.

CHAPTER ONE

A man could only take so much squealing.

Thomas was positive the noise level was going to drive him to insanity before he was thirty. He would never have believed little girls could be *so loud*. His carefully managed household had disintegrated into chaos in the past month.

There were stains on the dining room chairs where the children had spilled their food when he had mistakenly believed they could all sit round the table for a family meal. He had learned his lesson with that one. Now, they took their meals in the nursery. The four of them ran roughshod over the house, sliding down banisters and climbing the curtains. On the bright side, his banisters never needed polishing. But his curtains were in tatters.

So were his nerves.

He was looking forward with unbridled and unusual glee to a visit to his attorney that morning, a Mr. Phillips in Meryton. How he longed for adult conversation! To be somewhere quiet and peaceful! To complete a discussion without interruption!

It was all very much to be longed for and looked forward to with the greatest of expectations.

The door burst open and two little girls, followed closely by their brother, ran into his study.

"Uncle Thomas! Uncle Thomas! John pulled my hair!"

"I did not! You are lying!"

"Did too!"

"Did not!"

"Did too!"

Thomas rubbed his temples. Yes, a visit to the attorney was definitely in order. He was past ready to escape this madhouse for some civilized company!

*****

Mr. Philips was shocked speechless when the normally staid Thomas Bowen entered his office whistling merrily. He had never seen the man so at ease. He actually *lounged* in the armchair across from him.

He raised his eyebrows at the silly grin that spread across the younger man's face.

"If I did not know better," Mr. Phillips remarked, "I would think you in the midst of an infatuation. Has some young lady caught your eye at last?"

Thomas laughed, too pleased to be out of the house to let his attorney's assumptions bother him. "No. I am simply thrilled to be among adults. I never thought to be so glad for silence in my life. Those children have taken over my house, plain and simple, and I have no idea how to gain control again."

"They have been with you how long? A month? Surely it cannot be as bad as you say."

"If not, it is surely worse."

"Have you no governess to care for them while you carry out your business?"

Thomas sat straight up in his chair. "A governess? I had not thought of that! It is just the thing!" He looked thoughtful for a moment as hope briefly lit his face. But then he slumped back in his seat dejectedly. "Where am I to find a governess in Hertfordshire?" he bemoaned. "And quickly at that!"

Mr. Phillips took pity on the poor man. "Surely my wife would know of some suitable young lady. We are hosting a small dinner party this evening. Perhaps you might ask for suggestions there? If my wife cannot think of anyone, I have no doubt one of the other ladies present must know of someone."

Thomas frowned at the invitation. He normally avoided such social engagements as if they were a deadly disease. But desperate times called for desperate measures. He could place an ad in the papers, but that might take weeks, and he did not have the time to waste interviewing candidates.

No, one evening of discomfort was far more preferable. "I believe that would be most satisfactory."

Mr. Phillips informed him as to the details of the gathering and then they turned their attention to the business that had brought them there to begin with.

*****

Thomas checked his appearance one more time in the looking glass. His skin tingled with nerves and anticipation. He cleared his throat loudly and slid one finger under the collar that was suddenly choking him. Just as quickly, he tried to smooth his cravat back down. His valet would not be happy if he ruined all his careful work before anyone had seen it. The poor man had been thrilled at the opportunity to display his skills and dress his employer for a rare dinner party. Thomas had felt slightly guilty under the man's ministrations. His talents were sadly underutilized on him. He had almost wanted to reassure the man he would attend more social functions, just to make the poor chap feel his efforts were appreciated.

But he had stopped the words just in time, as he remembered the last fiasco of a ball that he had attended. He shuddered to think of his stammering replies and stilted dances. He had regaled one young lady with the entire history of the quadrille during their set, only to overhear her later making fun of him to her friend.

It had not been an enjoyable night. His only consolation was that he had not been the only one who had made a fool of himself at the Netherfield ball. It had seemed the whole of the Bennet family had subjected themselves to ridicule. Even their cousin, Mr. Collins, had made a complete idiot of himself, speaking so presumptuously to the illustrious Mr. Darcy, when he had not even been introduced to the man!

That had been almost four years ago now, and he had rarely ventured into society since.

He had tried to prepare himself for the evening to come, but already any confidence he might have possessed had dwindled into awkwardness. He sighed. Best be on with it. Waiting only made the task seem that much more formidable.

He descended the stairs to the waiting carriage below.

*****

Mrs. Phillips had been horrified by her husband's announcement that he had invited Mr. Bowen to their dinner party. "Why on earth would you invite *that man* to our home?! He can hardly be considered agreeable, and he is certainly not handsome! Even though he *does* have five thousand a year, all he does is drabble on about nothing at all!"

Mr. Phillips chuckled at his wife's effusions. "*That man*, as you so eloquently put it, is in desperate need of some female advice. I believed that you, with your extensive knowledge of the society in these parts, could be of assistance. Was I wrong to assume so?"

Mrs. Phillips puffed up at his words. "No! No! You are quite right. If there is anything to be known I shall know it. There is nothing that passes that escapes my notice. All of Meryton is aware that!"

"Then I was quite right to invite him to dine with us. You shall be of the utmost assistance to him."

"Of course I shall be!" she huffed. "He would not find better information in all of Hertfordshire!"

*****

Mrs. Phillips had put forth special effort to make Thomas feel welcome upon his arrival. She was pleased to have her opinion sought, and the compliment to her vanity far outweighed her prejudice against the man.

There was no time for private conversation before they all went in to dinner, so Thomas had to content himself with biding his time until tea was served. It was a difficult thing to do, given his dislike for social engagements in general, but he sought to make himself agreeable by conversing with Miss Long, who was seated to his right.

"Did you know, Miss Long, that the word dinner, as we know it now, is derived originally from the Latin word *disjējūnāre,* which meant to break one's fast? Of course, that is also where we derive the word breakfast. Not from *disjējūnāre*, I mean, but from breaking one's fast. I think breakfast is a decidedly boring word, do you not agree? It means exactly what it sounds like. There is no enjoyment in the discovery at all."

Miss Long looked up from where she had been prodding her peas about her plate. "I had no idea you were so, er… *knowledgeable*… on the matter, Mr. Bowen."

Thomas warmed to his subject. "Oh, yes. I find linguistics and etymology to be quite fascinating. The word etymology is itself quite diverting. It originates from two Greek words: *étymo,* meaning true, and *logos,* meaning word or reason. So, when put together, they mean true word or true reason. You see, then, how that clarifies the word, since you are looking for the true reason of the word, not a false or an assumed basis. Etymology therefore requires quite diligent study if you are to uncover the complete meaning and history of the word, because all one's assumptions must be pushed aside and the truth only must be carefully sought."

Thomas concluded his monologue enthusiastically, as it was one of his favorite subjects, only to come to the realization that Miss Long's eyes had long since glazed over, and although she was diligently nodding along to everything he said, her attention had drifted. Almost as soon as he had stopped speaking, she turned decidedly to her other dinner companion, engaging him with some town gossip she had overheard.

Thomas turned his attention to the lady on his left, hoping to converse with her, only to be met with the back of her head, as she was firmly engaged in speaking to the gentleman on her other side.

His cheeks flushed with two bright spots of pink as he came to the conclusion that both young ladies were pointedly avoiding talking to him. He lowered his head and applied himself to his meal in an effort to cover his embarrassment. He had done it again, despite his best intentions.

He should have known better than to bring up etymology. He had simply been trying to find a common ground to converse about. Surely, any accomplished young lady, as those around him claimed to be, would have been interested in acquiring knowledge. But, if the conversations around him held any evidence, the young ladies were more interested in acquiring and spreading the village gossip than pursuing knowledge.

He sighed and fiddled with his roast beef. He would never learn how to fit in with polite society.

After that debacle, dinner was just something to be endured and got through as quickly as possible. There could be no real enjoyment in the meal. Thomas felt some relief when the ladies adjourned to the parlor, leaving the gentlemen to their port. But even here, he was afraid to open his mouth, lest he should commit some further social gaffe, especially as the conversation drifted into topics he would prefer to leave untouched.

He shifted uncomfortably as the alcohol flowed liberally, loosening too many tongues. He sat stiffly through the men's ribald jokes and knowing winks, coughing at the cloud of cigar smoke that fogged the room.

When they were finally able to rejoin the ladies in the parlor, Thomas had developed a pounding headache and had no desire to do anything but obtain the information he needed and politely excuse himself. Even the noise at home was preferable to this.

To his delight, he was able to accomplish his objective with very little effort on his part. Mrs. Phillips, once tea had been served, sought him out.

"I have been informed, Mr. Bowen, that you have need of a lady's opinion," she said proudly, batting her eyes and preening. "How may I be of service?"

Thomas, while repulsed by her vain display, was not about to let the opportunity pass him by. He cleared his throat and wiped his sweaty palms on his pants. "Yes. Well. About a month ago, as you are probably aware, my sister died, and her husband being at sea, I, umm, *inherited* her children. I have found that I have no affinity for the children, and your husband suggested to me, just this morning, that I should acquire a governess. I at once agreed, but I have not the slightest idea where to obtain one on such short notice.

I was hoping you might know of some suitable young lady in the neighborhood. Just someone to come during the day and see to them."

Mrs. Phillips leaned back in her chair to ponder this perplexity. She tapped one long finger against her lips and tried to put on a brooding air. Immediately, a young lady sprang to mind, but she pretended to think a little longer, to make it seem like she had really given the matter serious thought.

"One of my nieces, Miss Mary Bennet, is said to be the most accomplished young lady in the neighborhood. She is not perhaps as beautiful or as gregarious as some of the other young ladies, but I believe she should suit your purposes exactly. You will find her most amiable and I believe she would appreciate an excuse to get out of the house."

Thomas thanked Mrs. Phillips for her valuable assistance and took his leave. As his carriage pulled away from the entry, he turned his mind to Miss Mary Bennet. He knew very little about the young lady in question.

He remembered briefly passing through the room as she played the pianoforte at the Netherfield Ball. Her choice of music had perhaps been a little off for the venue, but he remembered being impressed with her level of skill at the instrument. Other than that, he only had a vague impression of a quiet brunette, overshadowed by her more vivacious sisters.

But it was a start. For the first time, he felt hope that he could stop the downward spiral that had begun when his sister's children had first stepped foot into his home. He thought wistfully of a return to his structured lifestyle and harmony within the four walls of his home.

If Mary Bennet could give him that, he would be eternally grateful to her.

CHAPTER TWO

Thomas set off early the next day to pay a call on Mr. Bennet and discuss the possibility of acquiring his daughter's services as a governess. He prayed the man would not take offense to his inquiry and think that he was insinuating he could not provide well enough for his daughter, so that she should have to work.

It was a thin line he was walking, but he desperately needed the assistance, and if Miss Mary Bennet would not have him… the prospect loomed before him, dark and dismal. He shuddered.

*****

Mr. Bennet was a man that was easily amused with the follies of others. He was an intelligent man, witty and cynical, if not particularly studious. He was not intentionally cruel in his amusements, even if some on the receiving end of his humor found him to be so.

It was with great amusement therefore, and some confusion, that he received the bumbling Mr. Bowen. The man was quite obviously agitated, pacing before his desk with his hat in his hands and unable to summon the words to express more than the faintest of pleasantries.

Mr. Bennet smothered his smile and beckoned for the younger man to take a seat. "To what do I owe this great pleasure, Mr. Bowen? Have the pigs got out again?"

Thomas flushed. "No. No, they have not." He took a deep breath to settle his nerves and let forth a torrent of words in a sudden onslaught. "I have come because I need a governess. Not that any of your daughters need be a governess, but I desperately need a governess. I have got four children in my house and I do not know what to do with them. They are taking over. That is why I need a governess. And Mrs. Phillips said your daughter, Miss Bennet, is the most accomplished young lady in the neighborhood and that she would make a most excellent governess. And so I determined that I should see if I could have her. As a governess, I mean."

Mr. Bennet settled back in his seat to digest this information. "Four children?" He looked up to confirm he was correct, and Thomas nodded enthusiastically. Mr. Bennet went on, speaking under his breath, more to himself than for Thomas' benefit. "Yes. Quite right…sister died about a month ago, if I recall correctly. Hmmph."

Thomas nodded again, although Mr. Bennet seemed to have no interest in his input at all. The other man was silent for several minutes. Thomas felt the silence lengthening, stretching his already frazzled nerves taut as a bowstring, until he thought that if it should go on one moment longer, surely he would snap.

Thankfully, Mr. Bennet chose that moment to speak. "I think, Mr. Bowen, if you are to pursue my daughter as a governess, there are a few things we need to discuss. The first of them is I cannot make this decision for her. Only Mary can accurately weigh the ramifications of such a choice on her reputation and decide how she should like to proceed. I have made it a practice, Mr. Bowen, to never force my daughters into anything, with very rare exceptions. Secondly, I feel it only fair to warn you that my daughter, although occasionally exposed to my nephews and nieces, is not in the habit of interacting with children. I am not at all sure that she will suit your purposes, despite, or perhaps because of, her accomplishments."

Thomas was not at all sure what to make of this last statement, or the slightly sarcastic tone in which it was said, and thus chose to ignore it and address the rest of Mr. Bennet's concerns. "She shall be better qualified for the job than I am, which is my main concern. As long as I am able to carry out my duties without being interrupted, I shall be happy."

Mr. Bennet steepled his hands together and leaned forward in his seat. "I see I cannot dissuade you. You have my permission, then, to seek out my daughter and inquire as to her preferences. At this time of the day, she is most likely in the sitting room with a book. I shall take you to her." He rose and led the way out of the study, Thomas following eagerly behind him.

His interview with Mr. Bennet had been less painful than Thomas had imagined. He only hoped that Miss Bennet would be as obliging.

Mr. Bennet could no more imagine his daughter accepting Mr. Bowen's proposition than he could Mrs. Bennet showing a sudden interest in classical literature. Mary's studious nature was not at all disposed to the exuberance of children. She had never shown herself to have any maternal instincts or leanings. To think of her now as such was highly diverting, to his mind!

He almost chuckled as he opened the sitting room door for Mr. Bowen. It was so preposterous! "Mary," he called, as his daughter looked up at his entrance, "Mr. Bowen has come to speak with you."

She looked startled at this proclamation. Now he did chuckle to himself. His daughter was shocked to receive a visitor. No other young lady of his acquaintance would have reacted so to the announcement that a young man of no little means was there to see her. If only her mother were at home! He could only imagine the shenanigans that were sure to have taken place.

He was disappointed his humor should not be so fully realized, but alas! That lady had taken herself and her nerves into town to call on her sister. Still, there was much to be amused with yet. He could surely count on Mary's reply to the gentleman not to disappoint.

*****

Mary blinked, her mind whirling with confusion, as her visitor entered the room behind her father and took a nearby seat. She could not fathom why Thomas Bowen would want to see her.

She studied the man before her. She knew very little about him. Lydia had been fond of mocking his awkward manners in company, but then again, she had also been fond of taunting Mary for her quiet behavior.

He was perhaps five foot ten, with ruffled blonde hair and intelligent chocolate brown eyes. His nose was crooked where it had been broken as a teenager, marring what otherwise could have been considered good looks.

She recalled that he was only a few years older than her own twenty-two years, putting him at around twenty-seven. He looked young for his age, rumpled in a waistcoat and jacket that were too big for his slim frame, his cravat knotted haphazardly. She smiled at the thought of his valet, and the horror with which he would view his master if he could but see him now.

Unwittingly as it was, the sight of that gentle smile was enough to goad Thomas into speaking. "Miss Bennet," he began, "I have a very great favor to ask of you."

Mary raised one eyebrow questioningly, her eyes darting to her father in surprise. Mr. Bennet nodded reassuringly, suppressing the smile that threatened to appear, and kept his mouth shut as Thomas continued.

"I am aware that it is perhaps quite unorthodox to ask a lady such as yourself for such a thing, but I have been informed that you are a most accomplished young lady." He took a deep breath and leaned forward in his seat, and Mary could see the desperation in his face. "I have recently acquired the privilege of caring for my sister's four children and I am in need of a governess. Just someone to come during the day and see to the children's education and entertainment while I carry out my business. I would be most obliged if you would take the position."

Mary was gratified by the compliment he paid her in soliciting her services. It was always nice to know one's accomplishments were noticed. But accepting the position he offered her could be tantamount to admitting her father could not provide for her. That was certainly not the case, with all four of her sisters married off. Longbourn had never been so comfortably situated.

At the same time, she recognized the opportunity the position gave her. She would no longer be tied to home, at the mercy of her mother's "poor nerves." She could have a degree of independence, and a little extra pocket money of her own. The position would not necessitate her being away from the comforts of home. It would merely expand her horizons.

Still, there was a degree of comfort to be given up, and it was that thought that had Mary biting her lip and hesitating.

She had never been particularly good with children, that lot having always fallen to Jane or Elizabeth.

While she was used to her own quiet ways, she did possess that most useful of qualities when dealing with children-patience. It would be good practice for if she ever had a family of her own one day. Her mother may have given up hope of her ever marrying, but Mary had not given up on that dream yet.

She studied the man before her and made up her mind. She would help him, if for no other reason than it was the Christian thing to do. The poor man looked afraid to hope, but was cautiously optimistic anyway. She could not crush his spirit.

"It is not an easy thing you ask of me," Mary started. "I generally prefer my own company. But I can see that you are in very great need, and I am willing to use what talents I possess to be of assistance."

Mr. Bennet looked startled at this pronouncement, and Mary could not help but take a little perverse delight in having shocked him. Thomas' delight, however, was all she could have hoped for.

A great grin broke out across his face, lighting up his eyes and revealing a dimple in one cheek. Mary blinked as she was suddenly struck by the realization that Thomas Bowen was positively *handsome*. She would never have thought it, had she not seen him smile. He radiated confidence at her words, no more the awkward young man she knew. She felt herself flush as she dragged her eyes away from that dimple winking in his cheek.

It was impossible not to smile back at him. They sat there for the space of several minutes, neither speaking, just grinning ridiculously at each other, until Mr. Bennet broke the silence.

He cleared his throat. "Well, Mr. Bowen, it seems you have secured yourself a governess. Perhaps we should adjourn to my study to discuss the terms of my daughter's employment."

Thomas finally removed his gaze from Mary and turned his attention to her father. "Yes, of course," he murmured distractedly. He looked back at Mary. "I hope, Miss Bennet, that you will come meet the children before you begin your official employment. I am sure they would be delighted to make your acquaintance."

Mary acquiesced genially, and a date was set upon. Then the two men left her to discuss the actual business arrangements. Mary was slightly irked to be left out of those discussions, seeing how they concerned her more than they did her father, but the man would never believe she had the intelligence and wit to make those decisions for herself.

She remembered ruefully his once denoting Lydia and Kitty as the silliest girls in all of England, and knew he considered her among them as well. Lizzy he had respected, and Lizzy it was that he preferred.

She frowned and picked up her book. It was best not to dwell on their invariable differences. It only left her feeling lonely and forgotten, and she did not want to ruin what was turning out to be a promising day with such unpleasant ruminations.

*****

Thomas was still distracted by a whirlwind of emotions as he sat down across from Mr. Bennet's desk in his study. Among the chief of these was elation. He was elated that the children were no longer his sole concern, that he now had a helpmate and aide in their care, and that his home might finally return to some semblance of order.

Underneath that overwhelming joy laid an indistinguishable knowledge, an innate sense that something very important had just happened. He could not quite put his finger on it, and yet when his gaze had connected with Mary Bennet's clear green eyes, something inside him had clicked into place. It was unrecognizable, yet somehow *right*.

Thomas did not have time to dwell on the matter, for Mr. Bennet was already peppering him with questions and he had to struggle to catch up with the man.

At the end of their interview, the hour having grown late, Mr. Bennet invited the young man to stay to dinner with the family, and was delighted when he accepted. He rubbed his hands together gleefully and allowed a small smile to escape. He was inclined to believe that Mrs. Bennet would be most pleased with this new turn of events, and enthusiastic. Dinner was sure to be entertaining.

*****

If Thomas had known what he was getting into when he accepted Mr. Bennet's dinner invitation, he would have declined. In hindsight, he should have remembered Mrs. Bennet's well-known match-making attempts and enthusiastic, gossipy nature. They had always been on prominent display at any social engagement both families had ever attended. He had just always been spared such indignities by her intense efforts to marry off her other daughters. He would never do for Jane or Lydia, and so had been beneath her notice. But now, with only one daughter left to marry off, and not one she was particularly fond of at that, he was suddenly fair game.

He may not have been handsome enough for Jane or dashing enough for Lydia, but plain, quiet Mary did not merit a handsome, engaging husband.

Mrs. Bennet's attempts to throw them together were obvious. She seated them across from one another at dinner. "My Mary looks well, does she not, Mr. Bowen?" she entreated him, hoping to draw forth some compliment and secure his affections in Mary's favor.

Thomas looked up, startled, from where he had been applying himself to his soup, his gaze flying between the two women, unsure how to answer the one without offending the other. He chose to deliberately misunderstand the question. "Have you been ill, Miss Bennet? You appear to be quite recovered, if such was the case."

Mary did not look up from her soup. Her cheeks hot, she tried to ignore her mother's shenanigans. "I am in good health, Mr. Bowen. Thank you for your concern."

Mrs. Bennet was not to be put off. "Mary is quite accomplished at the pianoforte, you know. Just this morning, Mrs. Long was commenting on it. 'We must have Mary play for us at our next dinner party,' said she. Such compliments she paid her! Perhaps we can have her play after dinner so you may enjoy her playing as well."

Thomas darted another glance at the young lady in question. Her head was still bent over her bowl, but her hand trembled where she held her spoon. He could tell she found her mother's line of reasoning distressing. "I am sure that would be most pleasant, but unfortunately I must be off directly after dinner."

Mary shot Thomas a grateful glance. He warmed under her intent gaze and dropped his eyes bashfully. He was confused by the conflicting emotions running through him. He was repulsed by Mrs. Bennet's pushy nature and made uncomfortable by her matchmaking notions, but he was also strangely drawn to the timid Miss Bennet, who had yet to say more than a few sentences to him. He was pleased to have garnered her favor with his response to her mother.

"Oh?" Mrs. Bennet said, disappointed. "That is too bad. You should have enjoyed it very much, I am sure. Never mind then, you shall have the opportunity again, to be sure."

Thomas acknowledged this was likely to be true and was relieved when Mrs. Bennet changed the subject. Mr. Bennet chuckled lightly to himself at this, drawing everyone's attention briefly and making everything even more uncomfortable. Mrs. Bennet, however, was never one to be put off, and she immediately started back up where she had left off, covering over the awkward moment.

The Bennets saw him into his carriage not long afterwards. He was relieved when the carriage jerked forward and he could leave the Bennet family behind him. He found himself wishing irrationally for the mayhem of his own home. At least the children had no designs on his person, other than eating him out of house and home and ruining his draperies.

He could deal with that. But the manipulations of a matchmaking mama? That was beyond him. He shuddered at the thought of Mrs. Bennet as a potential mother-in-law. Mary Bennet seemed like a nice enough young lady, but he had enough problems to deal with trying to raise four young children without the additional stress of becoming involved in a courtship. And he was certainly not sure if any woman was worth the consequences of tying himself forever to the ridiculous Mrs. Bennet.

The journey was not far to his own home, and he had barely begun his ruminations, it seemed, before the trip was made. He climbed the steps, weary from his social exertions and ready to spend the next week at least not venturing outside his study door. He paused on the landing, where he generally would have turned off to seek his own quarters, debating, and then continued up the stairs to what was now considered the nursery.

The children had all been put to bed in his absence. He paused outside the door, listening to the silence and smiling a little to himself at the novelty of it, before he cracked open the door and peeked in. No one stirred at the noise, so he ventured farther inside.

They were all sleeping peacefully in the darkened room. John, at ten, and the only boy, slept on his stomach, one arm flung up over his head and the other hanging off the side of the bed, his fingers just grazing the floor. Thomas frowned slightly. The boy really was too old to be relegated to the nursery with his sisters. He probably should have been sent off to school, but Thomas could not bring himself to send him away when the poor boy had already had to face so many changes in his life. He was going to have to talk to the housekeeper about arranging separate sleeping quarters for the boy.

He moved on to the next bed, which was ostensibly considered eight-year-old Emilia's, but tonight, as was often the case, it was occupied by both Emilia and her younger sister Sophia. He had the sneaking suspicion that Sophia, at six, was having a harder time making the adjustment to her new home than her older sister. The older girl had one arm wrapped comfortingly around her little sister, and he could still make out the traces of tears on Sophia's little face. He sighed and turned away. Only time could heal some wounds.

Only little Helene was left now. He peered down at her tiny frame wrapped in her favorite blanket and smiled. The toddler required the least of his attention and yet demanded the most of it, all at the same time. He had managed to secure a nurse for her with relative ease. But the tot had an engaging smile and a magnetic personality that made her impossible to ignore.

He reached out a finger to caress her downy cheek and smiled tenderly as she turned her cheek into his palm. He might have originally begrudged his nieces and nephew their place in his life, but now he would not change it for the world.

They had wormed their way into his life and stolen a little piece of his heart. They could be noisy and destructive and they turned his home upside down, but they brought life into his crusty existence. Now, if only Mary Bennet could manage to wrangle some sort of control back from the chaos, his life would be complete.

He pulled the blanket up a little higher around Helene's waist and turned to leave. He paused at the door to take one last look at the sleeping children. He had a feeling that having Miss Bennet in their lives was going to change them forever, and, surprisingly, he was rather looking forward to it.

He closed the door behind himself and went to find his own chambers.

CHAPTER THREE

Change can be a difficult thing for anyone, but it is especially so for those used to their own company and quiet pursuits. Mary Bennet, although she longed for recognition, was not a woman to seek out attention for herself. She was used to being forgotten about and left to her own devices for hours on end.

It was quite a shock, therefore, to suddenly have her mother's full, undivided attention thrust upon her.

The morning of her visit to Kaverstow found Mrs. Bennet in Mary's bedroom at an ungodly hour.

"Hurry, Mary! You must get up! There is so much to be done before you can appear before Mr. Bowen!"

Mary pulled the covers over her head in an attempt to drown out her mother's shrill voice. It did not work. Her shrieks pierced the cloud of slumber that Mary clung to.

"Rise, Mary! What you do to my poor nerves! You simply must look your best for Mr. Bowen! It is going to take all the time we have and our combined efforts if you are to look half as pretty as Jane!"

The covers were rudely jerked off her and the curtains drawn back to let the bright morning light into the darkened room. Mary sat up reluctantly, shivering in the chilly room and squinting against the harsh light.

Mrs. Bennet recoiled at the sight of her, still rumpled and bedraggled from sleep, and ordered Hill to get a fire started in the grate while she went to root about in the wardrobe for a suitable gown.

Mary drew up her knees to her chest and tucked her toes under the hem of her nightdress. She rested her chin on her knees and turned her head to gaze wistfully out the window as her mother and the servants bustled about around her.

The peace of the quiet spring morning, full of hope and promise, beckoned to her, stretching its arms out to her in a silent plea. She longed to flee into its embrace, free from the grasping machinations of her mother. The wind whispered her name as it wafted past the window panes, calling to her lonely heart.

She was torn from her whimsical ruminations by her mother's gleeful chuckle. "Five thousand a year! I knew you could not be so accomplished for nothing!" Mrs. Bennet laid aside the gown she had chosen and tugged Mary out of bed. "Come, child! It is time to dress!"

A short while later, Mary was seated, a maid attending to her hair while her mother directed the process from her seat at the foot of the bed. Mary winced as the maid jerked her head roughly to one side. Her hair was fine and straight, and while she had a lot of it, no amount of brushing or styling could hide the fact that it was limp and lifeless. The silky strands refused to hold a curl and were forever escaping her pins to fall in wispy strands around her face.

She pitied the maid. There was nothing the poor woman could do to improve upon it, but her mother was determined and unyielding that she should try and succeed in the endeavor.

Mary studied her reflection in the looking glass while the maid poked and prodded her. She knew she was no classical beauty. While she might no longer be constantly compared to the beauty of her other sisters, the comments had been indelibly marked in her memory. She had been deemed plain too often to forget it.

Her features were dainty and ordinary, possessing neither great beauty nor extreme unattractiveness. Her only notable features were a pair of large, intelligent green eyes, fringed heavily with thick brown lashes. One would assume that such striking eyes would dance or be alight with laughter, but Mary had learned well how to veil her thoughts and emotions. A lifetime of being deemed nothing more than a silly, stupid girl had ensured that. She had learned not to express her own thoughts or opinions, as they would only be ridiculed. Instead, she had sought out more authoritative sources to quote. If she was to be mocked, at least it was not her own thoughts and opinions deemed to be so ridiculous.

Very few people, if any, saw through her façade. She was not one to let down her carefully built defenses and open herself up to shame and humiliation. She had had enough of that to last her a lifetime.

The maid jabbed her with one last pin and stepped back to allow Mrs. Bennet to survey her handiwork. She clucked over the simple style and mourned the lack of curl, but Mary smiled to herself, secretly pleased with the outcome. The lack of fuss suited her perfectly. Her tastes were not elaborate or fashionable, as her mother would have preferred them to be. She rose and quietly thanked the maid, slipping out the door before her mother could insist on her making another attempt.

Breakfast would not be ready for some time yet, so Mary sought out a favorite book and her pelisse and hurried out into the spring air before her mother could catch her. She smiled at the thought of her earlier daydreams and walked briskly until she was out of sight of the house.

It was a simple and easy thing, then, to find a pleasantly situated tree stump for a seat and to reflect on the beauty that surrounded her. She smiled softly. Spring was such a happy time of year, and this morning it seemed particularly lovely. While the morning air was still crisp with the bite of winter, she could feel the earth stirring and wakening around her.

The trill of a bird call and the gurgle of a nearby brook welcomed her into their presence. If she peered closely enough around her, she could make out the first buds already forming on the trees and the hint of flowers, ready to shoot forth from their winter abodes.

She felt a sort of kinship with the life around her. She too had been stilted in a dark and melancholy world that did not appreciate her beauty, but now she was ready to burst forth into the brightness of day, where she could grow and prosper.

She had come to appreciate better the offer Thomas had made her, as time had passed. Despite her mother's misguided efforts, she was looking forward to the day ahead. She had been stuck in her role, confined in what society and her parents expected of her. By taking Thomas' offer, she was breaking free of this mold and opening herself up to opportunities and challenges that could never have been hers otherwise.

It was terrifying and liberating, all at the same time. She had never really been viewed as more than an accessory before. She was Mrs. Bennet's daughter, or Lydia's sister, or Mrs. Phillip's niece. She was included by necessity, not by choice. They accepted her presence for her abilities, not for her person. Her mother needed her in the morning room as a companion, but she no more desired her conversation than she did Fordyce's sermons. Her Aunt Phillips and Lydia valued her skills at the pianoforte, but only because it fulfilled their own desire for dancing or music.

Here at last she was given the chance to stand on her own two feet, to be known and accepted on her own merits alone. Thomas Bowen did not want her as a governess because she was Mrs. Phillip's niece or Mr. Bennet's daughter. He wanted her because she was accomplished and he believed she could benefit his nieces and nephew. It was pleasant to have one's accomplishments recognized and valued by someone without ulterior motives.

The first tickle of nerves started in her stomach. She hoped she could live up to his expectations. Moreover, she hoped she could do a credible job by his children. She would rarely, if ever, be in company with Mr. Bowen, but she was to be constantly with the children. They were the ones she would have to make the biggest impression on.

She chewed on her bottom lip nervously. Would they like her? She certainly hoped so. She could only pray they would not be as disparaging and assuming towards her as their adult counterparts had been.

The time had passed quickly as she pondered these thoughts. A bright shaft of light fell across her unopened book, recalling her to the time and place. She looked up and noted the position of the sun in the sky. Breakfast would be served soon, and it was time she was headed back. Her mother would desire her presence in the drawing room. She could not escape that duty yet.

She rose and brushed her skirts of any debris, careful to check for dirt, and collected her book. The short jaunt back was not enough to prepare her for the flurry of activity in the house. She sidestepped the bustling servants and made her way to the breakfast room, helping herself to the buffet laid out to choose from. Her father was already seated, his plate nearly empty, enjoying a cup of coffee as he awaited her arrival.

"Well, Mary, I hope you are pleased with yourself. You have set your poor Mamma's nerves quite on edge."

Mary glanced up from her plate, but made no reply. Her father did not expect her to.

"While you are adjusting your ideas," he continued, "Let us return to Mr. Bowen. He seems to be a most conscientious and polite young man, if a touch coarse, and I do not doubt he will prove to be a valuable acquaintance."

"Mamma certainly seems to agree with you."

"And you do not?" Mr. Bennet chuckled lightly to himself. "Have you no wish to be married to a gentleman of five thousand a year? Your mother certainly seems to have thought it beyond you before this."

"I should not care if he had five thousand a year or five hundred. It matters naught to me when kindness and sensibility must be considered."

"Ah. Then he is all that a young man ought to be, excepting that he is not handsome of course. Young ladies do seem to put a great deal of importance on a gentleman's good looks."

Mary flushed. "I have no designs upon his person, Pappa, regardless of how Mamma may wish it. I shall see very little of the man and a great deal of his children. That is hardly anything to recommend me to him."

"I am glad to find you so sensible of your situation," Mr. Bennet stated. "I should dislike to find you with expectations that are unlikely to be fulfilled."

Mary was unsure how to respond to such a statement and so kept silent, wishing that her father would divert his attention elsewhere so that she might eat her meal in peace.

Happily, her mother appeared at that moment. Unhappily, Mary now became the focus of that woman's attentions, although escaping the further notice of her father, as he excused himself from the table at the appearance of Mrs. Bennet for the more pleasant confines of his study.

Thus uncomfortably engaged, it was not until the appointed time arrived for her visit that she was able to leave the company of that lady and retire to the relative quiet of the carriage.

The journey was not quite as long as she would have wished it to be in order to settle her nerves, but she met the halting of the carriage with relative calm. The home that greeted her as she stepped down was modest but charming. It was not much larger than her own, although having the good fortune to possess a sizable addition to one side. The grounds were manicured and well-kept, with a wide gravel drive. All of this spoke well of its master and the care and pride he took in his property. Mary was inclined to find Kaverstow quite perfect in its situation and charm, and could not find fault with it, despite Mr. Bowen's professions of it being overrun with children.

Mr. Bowen himself appeared in the doorway to greet her, and led her upstairs without hesitation to be introduced to the children she was to be in charge of.

Mary was met with four appraising gazes as she set foot in the nursery, and one mildly curious one. She smiled at the sight of the three older children lined up to meet her, and a toddler held securely in the nurse's arms. She was slightly taken aback to realize Mr. Bowen had one so young, having been under the impression that all the children were of school age, but she was pleased to note the presence of the nurse, recognizing that the woman was quite capable of caring for her charge.

The nurse was also pleased to make her acquaintance, and to finally have a governess in the household, as the responsibility for all the children had fallen on her in the absence of a governess. Still, she looked the plain young woman standing before her up and down, sizing her up with a doubtful eye.

Mary recognized the look, having had it turned upon her from various sources before. One corner of her mouth quirked up wryly. Even here, she was met with skepticism. She gave the nurse a curt nod and turned her attention to the children.

Three small, upturned faces regarded her seriously, and she could not withhold the gentle smile that settled over her face at the sight. She stepped forward and squatted down to match their height.

Thomas hastened to step in and introduce them. "Miss Bennet, these are my nieces, Emilia and Sophia, and their brother, John. The baby is Helene. Children, this is Miss Bennet, who is to be your new governess."

"It is a pleasure to make your acquaintance," all three children intoned, making their bows very prettily in an obviously rehearsed move.

Mary smothered her amusement and struggled to maintain a serious visage. In an attempt to remain sober, she reminded herself of the importance of her position and the role she would play in their lives. "It is my pleasure, as well. I hope we shall be able to get on very well together."

John studied her, a disgruntled gleam in his eye. Thomas recognized his belligerent attitude at the same time Mary did.

He eyed the young man and stated firmly, "They have assured me they will be on their best behavior for you." His tone brooked no defiance and John begrudgingly cast his gaze downward.

Mary nodded. "I should appreciate that very much. I am relieved to hear it." She knew it was unlikely that his statement would be so easily enforced once the children had been turned over to her care, but it was nice to know he was on her side.

They dawdled a little while longer in the nursery, the children taking turns acquainting Mary with their room and the various resources available to her therein, before she and Thomas repaired to his study to discuss his expectations for her employment.

Times were easily agreed upon and settled for her arrival and departure, and topics of study introduced and decided upon. There was only one matter left to discuss, and Thomas was not quite sure how to bring it up. He fiddled with his pen as he tried to summon the words.

Mary beat him to it. "I noticed that John does not seem particularly thrilled with my presence."

Thomas cleared his throat. "Yes, well, he seems to be under the impression that at ten years old he does not need a governess."

Mary smiled. The poor man really had no idea. "He is quite right, you know. Most young men of his age are either sent off to school or taught by their fathers. A governess, generally, is only hired for the benefit of the young ladies of a household."

Thomas was startled by this revelation, and the surprise was evident on his face. He was obviously lacking in knowledge when it came to raising children. He shook his head, slightly disgusted with himself. A natural-born father he was not. He was flummoxed as to how to respond.

Mary took pity on him. "Perhaps you could take over his education. Observing your interactions with your steward or learning how to balance ledgers are simple methods you can use to teach him skills he will need if he is ever to care for an estate of his own. It does require some of your time and effort, but perhaps after spending some time with you, he could join me and the girls for some exercise in the gardens. That would allow you time to finish any urgent business without distractions."

Thomas nodded. "I shall consider it." He would have to. He could not very well open the boy up to embarrassment and ridicule by relegating him to the schoolroom with the girls, now that he understood how it should be. He sighed and rubbed his forehead. There was so much more to this than he had ever imagined, and he was beginning to get the feeling that hiring a governess was not quite the easy fix he had thought it would be.

Miss Bennet smiled understandingly at him from across the table. "It will become easier with time, I am sure. Once we have established a routine things will begin to fall into place."

"I certainly hope so. I cannot imagine them continuing as they have been for much longer."

They wrapped up their discussion and Thomas saw her into her carriage. "I will see you on Monday."

Mary nodded. "Yes. I will be here." She sat back against the seat as the carriage started forward. Her gaze was immediately drawn out the window and her thoughts turned inward. It had been a short visit, but an effective one. Some misunderstandings had been cleared up, and the children had been friendly, for the most part. Everything seemed to be properly in order. She found she was quite looking forward to Monday.

*****

Thomas rocked back on his heels and watched Miss Bennet's carriage disappear down the lane. He ran an agitated hand through his hair. Everything he thought he knew about his life had been thrown out the window. Again.

He sighed and turned to go inside as the trees concealed the carriage from view. He needed to figure out what he was going to do with John.

*****

Three little faces watched Miss Bennet's departure, unnoticed, from an upstairs window.

"I don't like her," John declared roundly. "She looks mean."

"Well, *I* like her, and so does Sophia!" Emilia retorted defiantly. "She has kind eyes, like Mamma did."

John snorted. "You are such a silly girl! You cannot tell anything from someone's *eyes*."

Emilia planted her fists on her hips and leaned forward menacingly. "Oh yeah? And I suppose you can tell she is mean just from her gown and the way she does her hair?" She poked his scrawny chest with one chubby index finger. "Mamma always said not to judge someone by how they look. She said the nicest people are often those we least expect to be so. You should be ashamed of yourself!"

For a moment, it seemed that John's bravado would wither under her demanding gaze and the reminder of their mother, but then he turned away defiantly. "We'll see who's right when she comes on Monday! Then you babies had better not come crying to me!" He stalked out of the room, slamming the door hard behind him, his steps loud on the stairs.

Sophia looked up at Emilia with wide eyes. "You don't really think she will be mean, do you?"

Emilia put one arm comfortingly around her sister's slender shoulders. "No. Of course not. Uncle Thomas would never get someone mean to be our governess."

"Do you think Uncle Thomas likes us?" Sophia asked worriedly. "Sometimes he doesn't seem happy when we come downstairs."

Emilia sighed heavily. "I'm sure in his own way he loves us. I just don't think he is used to children, Sophia. Mamma would never have asked him to take care of us if he didn't."

"But if he likes us, why did he go and get us a governess? Doesn't he want to spend time with us?" There was a hint of hurt in the little girl's voice and Emilia patted her shoulder comfortingly.

"Sure he wants to spend time with us. Otherwise he would have got us a live-in governess. He just wants us to grow up to be proper young ladies, so he can be proud of us."

Sophia's little chest puffed up. "I can make Uncle Thomas proud. I'll be a perfect lady."

"We both will." Emilia turned her attention back out the window, her thoughts far away. "Just like we promised Mamma." They were both silent for a moment, caught up in memories of the painful day they had made those promises. Then Emilia shook off the melancholy recollections and dredged up a smile. "Come on, Sophia, let's go outside and play."

CHAPTER FOUR

It is not always easy to define the truth of a matter.

It was true that Thomas eagerly awaited Miss Bennet's arrival Monday morning. It was also true that he felt compelled, as a gentleman, to greet her at the door and see her up to the schoolroom. But the reasons behind such feelings? That truth was not so readily discernible.

Because the truth of the matter was, he could have just as easily secluded himself in his study and let his butler, Bertram, see to her. In fact, this may have even been the most acceptable choice, as she was now considered an employee in his household. But for some reason, Thomas could not bring himself to treat Miss Bennet so callously. He wanted her to know he appreciated her efforts in his behalf. And he was excited to outline to her the steps he had taken for John's education. And if he chose not to examine the truth behind such reasoning too closely, well, that was his business.

For perhaps the first time in his life, Thomas was glad polite society had shunned him. He did not have to worry about what people would think of him for associating with the hired help, or what would be expected of him in this situation. He could simply do as he pleased and act in whatever manner suited him. The local society could hardly make him more of a social outcast than he already was.

So it was, therefore, that Thomas watched Mary Bennet alight from her carriage with a surprising lightness of heart. He came forward as her feet touched the ground, a huge grin on his face. "Miss Bennet, it is a pleasure to have you. I trust your journey was not too arduous."

Mary was slightly taken aback by his buoyant mood, and, as the journey was not above a few miles, could not help but respond with an answering smile. "I thank you, it was not. My father could spare the carriage for me this morning. In the future though, I should enjoy the walk, so long as the weather is fine."

Thomas offered her his arm, which she accepted, and they began walking towards the house. "I should hope your father would not expect you to go on foot should the weather turn bad. It is a pretty little distance to walk."

"As long as the horses are not needed elsewhere, he will not begrudge me the carriage." Aware they were treading towards a somewhat dangerous topic, as Mrs. Bennet would quite happily deny her the carriage if it necessitated her staying at Kaverstow longer, Mary steered the conversation into a safer direction. "Have you decided on a course of action for John's education?"

He had, and he was eager to discuss it with her and ascertain her opinion. Their steps slowed as they talked, until they were standing still in the entry, engrossed in their conversation.

Three pairs of eyes and ears peered down at them over the balustrade, straining to make out their discussion.

"What do you think they're talking about?" asked Sophia.

"Grown up stuff," replied Emilia.

John snorted derisively. "You girls are so silly. They're talking 'bout us, obviously."

"Well, I wish they'd hurry up and finish," Sophia complained. "I'm bored."

"You're always bored," John said irritably, as he shifted to get a better view of the entry.

Sophia pouted. "Am not!"

"Are too!"

"Am not!" She punctuated her words with a shove, sending him careening into a plant stand. The heavy stand went toppling over, covering John in dirt and debris, while the noise echoed in the marble entry. The children froze, eying each other guiltily before edging closer to the railing to peek over and see if they had been caught.

It was a bit too much commotion to go unnoticed. Mary and Thomas had both turned and were looking up towards the source of all the noise. At the first sign of the culprits, Thomas sighed. "You might as well come on down," he advised them.

Hesitantly, they emerged from the shadows and descended the stairs to stand before them. Thomas grimaced at the sight of John, covered in dirt from head to toe, with bits of leaves and twigs sticking out of his hair. It was not the impression he wanted Miss Bennet to have of the children.

Thomas scrubbed one hand over his face, his buoyant mood evaporating. He really did not want to have to deal with this right now. "What happened?"

He was met by three perfectly innocent blank faces. "Nothing," they chorused.

Thomas was not fooled. "Someone had better own up to this, or there will be no dessert for any of you tonight."

Sophia squirmed and Thomas pounced, identifying the weak link as the one with the notorious sweet tooth. "Sophia, what happened?"

She sent her brother and sister apologetic looks. "John said something mean and I pushed him and he fell into the plant stand and knocked it over. But it is all his fault!" She pointed at her brother in an attempt to lay the blame at his feet.

"John should not have said mean things," Thomas agreed. "But that is no reason to push your brother. Now tell each other you are sorry."

Begrudgingly, they followed his instructions.

"Now, John, please go upstairs and clean up, then join me in my study. Girls, Miss Bennet will be up in five minutes to join you in the schoolroom. I expect you both to be waiting patiently in your seats when she arrives."

They all scampered off to do as he bid, relieved to be off the hook so easily.

He looked back at Mary apologetically. "I am afraid this is not quite the beginning I had hoped for. The children can be quite rambunctious, for which I do apologize. I fear this does not bode well for what is to come."

Mary Bennet just smiled. "You forget, Mr. Bowen, that I grew up as one of five sisters. This is nothing." She curtsied and started towards the stairs, pausing on the first step to call back over her shoulder, "I thank you for the escort, Mr. Bowen, and the warning. But I think I shall be fine from here."

Thomas watched her ascend the stairs in a state of shocked disbelief before, inadvertently, a huge grin broke out over his face. Now that was a woman!

*****

Some time later, Thomas heard footsteps in the hall outside his study door. He paused in his accounting, his pen still poised over the paper as he waited for the knock at the door. Thirty seconds passed without a sound, and he smiled as he imagined John on the other side of the door, straightening his clothes and screwing up the courage to face his uncle.

Finally, the rapid tattoo of John's knock sounded at the door and Thomas replaced his pen, composing his face into an indecipherable mask. He called, "Come in!"

The door squeaked open and John edged hesitantly around it to come stand before Thomas. The boy shifted nervously, his eyes darting around the room, looking everywhere but at his uncle.

Thomas sighed and gestured to the chair in front of his desk. "Please sit down, John. We have some things to discuss."

John was not quite sure what to make of such a statement. He settled warily into his seat, unsure if he was still to be punished or if he was in the clear for the little debacle on the landing that morning.

Thomas leaned forward, resting his weight on his elbows. "Miss Bennet has brought it to my attention that young men, such as yourself, have no need of a governess. I apologize for failing to recognize this and for treating you as if you were one of your sisters. It was done in ignorance. Thus, I have taken on the task of your education myself. I had planned on taking you with me to inspect the fields this morning." Thomas paused as John leaned forward eagerly, his eyes lighting up at the prospect of an excursion. "But after the scene you and your sisters caused this morning, and the resulting cleanup, we no longer have the time. So, you are to have a lesson in the ledgers instead."

Thomas felt guilty as the words left his mouth and the light faded from his nephew's eyes. He hastened to add, "But if you behave yourself properly, and show up promptly for your lessons tomorrow morning, there is no reason why we cannot ride out then." He was relieved when a wide grin reappeared on John's face.

This parenting thing was harder than it looked. He had to balance his desire to make them happy with what he knew was best for them in the long run. It was a hard line to walk, especially when they looked at him the way John was now.

For one agonizing moment he debated giving in and taking the boy out to the fields anyway. Then he firmed his resolve. Giving in to the children was part of the reason his household was in the state it was in now. He had to be the adult.

He rubbed a hand over his face in an effort to break the hold John's eyes had over him and instructed the boy to pull up his chair beside him so they could go over the ledgers. It was going to be a long couple of hours.

*****

By the time luncheon rolled around, Mary was quite pleased with the progress she had made with Emilia and Sophia. The girls had both been sweet and attentive and she had been able to determine a baseline for where both girls had left off in their studies before the death of their mother.

They took a break for the midday meal. Their meal was simple fast, just some bread and cheese and cold cuts, but it was enough to reenergize them for the afternoon ahead. *Perhaps a little too much,* Mary thought, as the girls fidgeted in their seats and she had to recall their attention back to their books.

Finally, she grew tired of fighting for their attention. She closed her book abruptly and stood, startling Emilia and Sophia back from their daydreams.

"I think it is time for a break," she stated firmly. "Shall we move outside for some play time?"

The girls immediately cheered up at the prospect. They rushed to put on their coats and hats, as it was still a little nippy out, and Mary let them precede her down the stairs.

On their way down they ran into the nurse, carrying a just woken Helene outside for some exercise of her own. The woman looked haggard, and Mary could only imagine that the toddler's nap time had not been the welcome respite the woman had hoped for.

Taking pity on her, Mary offered to take the child outside with her, since that was where she was headed anyway. The relieved woman eagerly handed over her burden and disappeared upstairs.

With the girls waiting for her at the bottom of the stairs, Mary settled Helene against her shoulder and carefully descended the stairs to join them. They made their way out into the gardens, where Mary found a comfortable bench to sit on while the girls chased each other around the plants.

Helene was still sleepy enough to want to snuggle. She settled into the crook of Mary's arm and popped her thumb into her mouth, making herself comfortable on her lap. Mary could not help but smile at the feel of the warm little body cuddled into her arms. It was an unexpected pleasure. Having been raised in a household of women, she had rarely had the fortune to be relegated to baby holding. That lot had naturally fallen to Jane or Lizzy, with her mother or aunt occasionally monopolizing the task. She had never really understood the appeal until now, when the opportunity was handed to her.

There was just something so *right* about holding a child in her arms. It was undeniable and yet foreign, all at the same time. She had never felt herself to be maternal, but so it was. She wondered at it briefly, then found herself obligated to turn her attention back to the frolicking girls as they threatened to wander too far away.

They heeded her call begrudgingly, having grown used to roaming the property without an adult's presence. She sighed as they resumed their play. So much damage had been done in one month. Wresting control back was going to take some time, despite the respect they already afforded her. There was still so much for them to learn.

*****

Thomas was wondering how long the peace and quiet in his house could last when the sound of laughter floating on the breeze filtered through his window.

John was still bent diligently over the ledger, intent on the tasks Thomas had set him, so he crossed the room to peek out the window and see what was going on. The sight that greeted him was a pleasant one.

The girls were outside playing. Mary Bennet sat on a bench to one side, overseeing their exercise, with Helene bundled up on her lap. The scene was so pleasant and jovial that Thomas could not help but long to join them. He cast a calculating glance over at his nephew and noted he was shifting in his seat and glancing up furtively. The boy was getting antsy, and to own the truth, so was he. His study might be his sanctuary, but it only functioned as such when he had it to himself.

He made up his mind. "Finish the page you are on John, and then let us take a break. I think some time in the gardens might be in order."

The boy was thrilled by the prospect and immediately applied himself to finishing the page. Thomas was surprised by the speed in which he completed the work, and then chuckled to himself as John raced to collect his coat before going outside. There was nothing like the prospect of fun to motivate a young man. He was sure John's finished product was full of miscalculations and errors, but it could wait until they returned. The lessons on the merit of thoroughness and accuracy over speed would keep for another day.

He fetched his own overcoat at a more leisurely pace, smiling to himself at his nephew's youthful enthusiasm. John was waiting impatiently for him on the landing when he returned.

"Come on, Uncle Thomas!" John cried anxiously. "If we don't hurry the girls will be in before we go out!"

Thomas led the way down the stairs. "I did not realize you were so attached to your sisters."

John was flummoxed, unwilling to admit to desiring his sisters' company, and yet unable to deny it without being labeled a liar. He grumbled under his breath at his uncle's back as he followed him down the stairs.

Thomas smiled at the noise and kept on going, holding the door open for John to precede him outside before following sedately behind him.

The boy ran to join his sisters in a game of hide-and-go-seek, while Thomas was content to join Miss Bennet on the bench and watch them play.

Miss Bennet smiled welcomingly as he approached. "I see your pupil was just as eager as mine were for some time outdoors."

Thomas settled on to the bench beside her. "Yes. It seems after luncheon is not a particularly productive time of day for children."

Miss Bennet laughed lightly, the trill of its cadence entrancing him. "We may be forced to make this into a permanent play time if we expect to be able to make any progress in the afternoons."

"You may be right," Thomas agreed.

Helene had perked up at her uncle's appearance and was now clamoring to be let down. Mary let her go reluctantly, immediately missing the warmth and comfort of the toddler's round body against her side.

Helene only took a few steps once she was set on the ground to come to stand before Thomas, lifting her arms to be held and smiling bewitchingly at her uncle, a dimple flashing in one cheek. Thomas laughed and accepted her invitation, lifting her up on to his lap.

Mary looked between the two, noting the identical dimple that winked in Thomas' cheek as he grinned at his niece. The family resemblance was uncanny. She thought wistfully of that grin being directed towards her, and then shook herself free of her errant thoughts and back to reality with a light blush as Thomas began speaking.

"We are fortunate Helene woke up in time to join us as well," he said, tickling the toddler playfully.

The little girl giggled and popped her thumb into her mouth, settling happily against Thomas' chest and watching her siblings play.

"She looks so much like her mother," Thomas added with a sigh. "They all do."

"You must miss your sister very much," Mary replied carefully, hoping she said the right thing. It was a delicate topic, and she did not want to trample on his feelings or assume wrongly.

Thomas shrugged. "She had been married and in Portsmouth for so long… It almost does not even seem real. Like she is still back there, waiting for her husband to come home." He bounced Helene lightly on his knees, eliciting a small smile around her thumb.

"Surely having the children here makes it more real."

"Yes. Although it is difficult to believe this is my new reality. Somehow, I always thought I would have time to go down and visit and be an uncle, but in truth I never had the occasion to." He paused in his speech to turn his gaze back to Mary. "No. That is not true. If I am honest, I never made the time to. There was always something more pressing that had to be done." He sighed and ran one hand over his face. "They had never even met me before I arrived to take them home with me."

Mary's eyebrows shot up in surprise. "I see now why you were in such desperate need of a governess."

Thomas laughed outright at her frank comment. "Yes. If I am quite hopeless as an uncle, how much less so must I be as a guardian!"

Mary's gaze softened as she regarded him. "I do not think you are hopeless as an uncle, much less as a guardian. It will just take some time to fill the role."

The look in Mary's eyes very nearly took Thomas' breath away. For a long, intense moment neither looked away. Then Mary turned her head and cleared her throat uncomfortably. "After all, most parents are given some months to adjust to the idea of a new child. You had four thrust upon you instantly."

"Yes, well, now I have a governess to help me out, so I expect things to become immeasurably easier," Thomas teased.

Mary smiled. "As much as I appreciate your faith in my skills, I would not count on that if I were you. I have precious little experience myself."

"Ah, yes, but more so than I do, which is the important thing to note. Already I am impressed with your talents."

Mary blushed. "I have done nothing out of the ordinary, I assure you."

"I beg to disagree. My house has not known such peace and quiet for a month. Helene thanks you, I am sure, as well, for there has been so much turmoil since she has arrived that her daily naps had all but disappeared."

"It is very important for young ladies to get their rest at this age. I imagine that a lack of a nap only added to the noise."

"It certainly did not help."

Helene interrupted them by popping her thumb out of her mouth long enough to point at the gardens and say, "Don."

Both adults looked down at her in confusion. "Don?" Thomas asked. "What does that mean?"

Mary shrugged. "I have no idea. Do you know anyone named Donald or called Don?"

"Don!" Helene insisted impatiently. "Bub."

Thomas sighed. "I can speak Latin, Greek, French, and Italian- all the modern languages- but I need a translator for a baby."

Mary smiled at his statement as Helene continued to point determinedly. "I think perhaps she is just as frustrated with our inability to understand as we are with her inability to communicate."

The little girl transferred her gaze from the gardens to Mary and stated irritably, "Don. Bye-bye!"

Mary frowned. "Bye-bye?" She jumped up from her seat, suddenly horrified, as the meaning of Helene's words washed over her. "John! She means John!" Her heart fell as she cast a harried glance over the gardens before them. The three older children were nowhere to be found. She had become so engaged in her conversation with Mr. Bowen that she had neglected to pay attention to her charges.

She should have known a game of hide-and-seek was not a good idea, especially when the girls had already shown a penchant for wandering off! She began to wring her hands fretfully. This was not a good way to begin her employment! What kind of governess was she? How was the man going to react when he realized she had lost his children?

Thomas reached one hand up to calm the suddenly hysterical Miss Bennet with a pat on the arm. "Miss Bennet, whatever are you talking about? What is this about John? He is just over there, playing with his sisters."

Miss Bennet turned horrified eyes upon him. "That is just it, Mr. Bowen, he is not! None of them are! I have lost your children!"

And then the normally composed Miss Mary Bennet burst into tears.

CHAPTER FIVE

Thomas must have sat there in shock for a full minute before he managed to gather his wits about him enough to say or do anything. Mary Bennet had collapsed, weeping, with her head in her hands, on to the bench beside him. He shifted Helene to one side and awkwardly patted Miss Bennet on the shoulder.

"There, there, Miss Bennet," he said uncomfortably. "I am sure the children are fine. This is not the first time they have disappeared like this. In fact, sometimes I think they do it on purpose, just to annoy me." He smiled unconvincingly, trying to inject some humor into the situation. It did not work. Mary Bennet just sobbed harder.

He cleared his throat. "You are not the only one to blame here. I should have been paying attention to their whereabouts more closely as well. I am sure that if we search they cannot have wandered too far."

Mary Bennet sniffled and wiped her eyes. "Are you sure you are not mad?"

Thomas smiled, relieved to see her gathering her composure once again. Handling a crying woman was beyond his capabilities. "I am."

She graced him with a watery smile, and he realized with a start that his hand was still on her shoulder. He pulled it away hurriedly and wrapped it securely around Helene in an attempt to keep himself from reaching out to touch Miss Bennet again. His fingers itched with a strange urge to wipe the tears from her porcelain cheeks. He was confused by the sudden compulsion to comfort her, and rose to distract himself from such perplexing emotions.

"We had better begin searching before they get too far. Are you up for a walk, Miss Bennet?"

Mary took the hand he held out to help her off the bench. "Of course. A little exercise will do me some good."

He settled Helene in his arms and set off with quick strides. Mary scrambled to catch up with him, her short legs scurrying as fast as they could to keep up. She loathed the family genes that had rendered her and her sisters on the petite side, except for the fortunate Lydia, who was the tallest by several inches despite being the youngest.

Thomas was oblivious to her plight, focused as he was on scanning the shrubbery for little faces and listening intently for the sound of little girls' giggling. This was not the first time he had been forced to roam his property in search of his nieces and nephew. They had begun exploring almost immediately upon their arrival at Kaverstow and were forever disappearing off to some hiding place or another they had discovered, sending the servants into a panic and dragging him away from his work in order to find them. He had hoped these bids for his attention would cease with the arrival of Miss Bennet, but it appeared that this was not the case. At least not yet. He sighed. It was going to be a longer transition than he had originally thought.

He glanced back over his shoulder to advise Miss Bennet to alert him should she see any movement in the bushes and noticed she was lagging a good twenty yards behind. Guiltily, he realized he was fast outpacing her, and slowed his gait so she could catch up. He did not miss the look of relief on her face when she came up even with him, but surprisingly, there was no admonition for him on her lips.

He apologized anyway, then led the way to one of the children's hiding places that he had discovered, careful to shorten his strides so Miss Bennet could keep up.

He held back a low hanging tree branch so she could pass underneath and then pointed to the opening of a small cave in the hillside. "This is one of the first hiding places they discovered after they arrived. They do not use it as often anymore since I have found it, but I thought I would check here first as it is the closest to the house."

Mary eyed the mouth of the cave warily. "Is it safe to go in there?"

Thomas took pity on her since it was obvious she had no desire to go in herself. "Yes. This area is perfectly stable and the cave is not large. But you may remain out here, if you prefer, while I investigate."

The look on her face was almost comical in its relief. "I should prefer that very much. I find small, dark places very distasteful."

He handed off Helene to her and went to inspect the cave, stooping to squeeze into the tight opening and disappearing into the darkness.

Mary shifted back and forth on her feet as she waited for Thomas to reappear. "Your uncle is a very brave man," she informed Helene, her nerves exhibiting themselves in the form of a rambling monologue. "All those spiders and creepy things." She shuddered. "And the possibility of bats! You will never see me going in there, I assure you."

Thomas' blonde head resurfaced. "Well, they are not in there." The rest of him followed, looking a little worse for wear. Mud stained the knees of his trousers and his hair was disheveled where he had scraped his head on the roof of the cave, but none of this mattered to Mary. She was inordinately pleased to see him returning safely to her.

The overwhelming delight bewildered her, having rarely experienced such strong emotions before, especially towards a near stranger. She tamped down the surge of emotion and struggled to greet him with a cool smile. The man was her employer, after all. "I suppose there are other places you are aware of that we can check as well?"

He took Helene from where Mary had settled her on her hip. "Yes, but they are all further out." He sighed. "I cannot believe they have covered so much distance in so little time."

Mary smiled. "It is amazing the energy and stamina God has bestowed in such little packages. I wish he had granted me half what he has given them."

Thomas laughed. "That would be a blessing indeed!"

Mary grinned back at him, lost in his amused gaze and happy to have been the one to put a smile on his face. Thomas cleared his throat after several moments had ticked by in such a fashion and the silence threatened to extend. "Well, I suppose we had best get moving if we are to have any chance of catching up with the children."

Mary quickly agreed, and they set off once again, traipsing deeper into the park. Mary lengthened her strides as much as she could so she would not hold Thomas back. She could not help feeling that she was some hindrance to him, with her paltry, short legs.

At the same time, though, it was important that she accompany him, should the children disappear when he was not around to search with her. She shivered at the thought, all the while knowing it was a distinct possibility. The man had hired her with the hope that she would take care of his children so he could concentrate on his own estate business. She knew her own father was frequently out of the house, inspecting fields and meeting with his tenants. Mr. Bowen was not always going to be around to bail her out of her messes. She was going to have to learn how to stand on her own two feet as a governess. She only hoped the learning curve was not too steep.

She nearly tripped over a tree root trying to keep up with Thomas' pace. He halted immediately, and reached out one hand to steady her, the other arm still wrapped securely around Helene. Mary was surprised by the strength of his grip. He flushed as he caught her staring and let go of her hastily. "It is just a little farther now. Watch your step."

Soon after, the outline of a hermitage appeared in the underbrush. It was little more than an overgrown hut in the woods, but Thomas hurried to assure Mary that it was currently uninhabited.

They looked at each other and smiled as the faint strains of girlish laughter reached their ears. "Maybe not completely uninhabited," Thomas amended with a grin. They hurried forward, intent on nabbing their prey now that they were within range.

They threw open the door, Thomas crying out a loud, "Aha!"

The three children jumped, startled by their sudden presence, and immediately looked overcome with guilt at being caught.

Mary shook her head at their change of heart. A moment earlier they had been laughing, enjoying their escapade with no thought for the repercussions of their actions. Surely they must know by now, especially given Thomas' reassurances that this was somewhat of a regular occurrence, that there were consequences for taking advantage of their inattention and sneaking off like that.

Thomas gestured for all of them to come out, and they slunk back through the door, heads hung low. Mary half expected him to launch into a tirade as they lined up outside, but he did nothing more than order them back to the house. She snuck glances at him as they marched the children back, wondering.

Even as inexperienced as she was, she knew children needed rules and consequences if they chose to break those rules. Surely, Mr. Bowen had put rules in place for them. He must have. Right? She suddenly was not so confident that he had.

She had a sneaking suspicion they would never have been allowed to get away with such behavior had their mother still been alive to see it.

The children began to drag their feet as they neared the house. She shook her head at their pathetic excuses. They had been left to their own devices for far too long. It was amazing how a lack of discipline could so easily undo all the hard work of a parent. She would have to speak to Mr. Bowen about setting some guidelines and putting consequences in place if she was to remain in control whatsoever. She must be able to exert her authority, or her pupils would soon discover the sham for what it was.

They ushered the children inside, and Mary sent the girls scrambling up the stairs ahead of her. She turned to Thomas and held out her arms to relieve him of Helene. "I will take her back up to the nursemaid, since I am going up anyway."

He handed over his burden, reluctant to part ways. Despite the aggravations, it had been an enjoyable afternoon, traversing his property with Mary Bennet by his side. Her cheeks and the tip of her nose were flushed a most becoming pink from the exercise and the lingering chill in the air. There was a sparkle in her eyes he had failed to notice before. The combination was enough to make him wish their traipse had lasted a little longer. She, however, did not seem to be of the same mindset.

She took Helene brusquely from his arms and started up the stairs without a backwards glance. A discussion on his disciplinary methods would have to wait for another time, when her duties as a governess did not have to take priority.

*****

Having handed Helene off to her nursemaid, Mary turned her attention to helping Emilia and Sophia out of their outerwear. Boots and coats were quickly discarded in favor of pinafores and slippers. Once the girls were suitably clad for their indoor activities, Mary sat them down for a little serious conversation.

"I am given to understand, girls, by Mr. Bowen, that today is not an isolated incident. I want to clear up any misunderstandings before we proceed further. I will not tolerate any repeats of today's performance. Should you decide to run off again, we will no longer be able to take a break from our lessons after lunch to play outside. Is that clear?"

The sisters shared a glance and replied in unison, "Yes, ma'am."

Mary considered them carefully, watching for any signs of deceit or disrespect, but found none. She sighed and pushed herself back up on to her feet. She was not sure what to think. She had been continually reassured by both the girls and their uncle that they would behave, and yet at the slightest opening they had taken off. Maybe they just did not know what the word 'behave' really meant. She shook her head. Then again, if there were not any rules in place, they probably had no idea what was expected of them. She had better have that discussion with Mr. Bowen sooner rather than later.

She turned her attention to the task at hand, pulling out a sewing kit for the girls. "Let us focus on your samplers."

*****

At the end of the day, just before her father's carriage arrived to bring her home, Mary Bennet trod lightly down one of Kaverstow's hallways to pause outside Mr. Bowen's study door. She screwed up her face with distaste at the unpleasant business set before her.

She disliked confrontation. But what must be said, must be said, and she was the only one who had the gall and the rank to be able to say it. No mere servant would ever dare to second-guess the master. A lady, on the other hand, might present her opinions and hope the master appreciated her insight.

Mary smiled wryly. Hope was the right word. She had not been respected by a male figure in her life since she was a child. She prayed Mr. Bowen was a different man than her father. She knew her ideas had merit. But would he think so?

She straightened her shoulders and stiffened her spine, lifting her chin to display confidence, even as she quaked inside. She could do naught but try.

She lifted one hand and rapped sharply on the solid oak door. There was a pause for what felt like ages but what was in reality probably only a few seconds. Then Mr. Bowen's voice called out, "Come in!"

She took a deep breath to calm the butterflies dancing in her stomach and pushed the door open.

Thomas looked up from his ledgers, John long since having been dismissed to pursue his own amusements. "Miss Bennet. This is a surprise. Please, do have a seat."

Mary blushed a comely shade of pink and took the seat he gestured to in front of his large, intimidating desk. She twisted her fingers in her lap, unsure of how to begin.

He folded his hands and smiled at her and suddenly the expanse of desk that stretched between them did not seem quite so imposing. "How was your first day?" he asked. "I thought it went tremendously."

"It went very well, all things considered. The only drawback was our lengthy excursion in the park. That, in a round-about way, is what has brought me to your study."

He cocked an eyebrow and rested his chin on his hands. "Is that so?"

She swallowed hard before plowing ahead. "It occurred to me on our walk back to the house that there do not seem to be any rules or consequences in place for the children. Is this correct?"

Surprise registered on Thomas' face at her inquiry. "I guess I have never put anything officially in place."

"I think it would be wise to do so now. Perhaps you can think over what you would like to implement and let me know what you decide. It would make my job much easier if I had something to enforce and the authority to do so."

To her surprise, Thomas seemed to take her suggestion seriously. He thanked her for her insight and promised to mull it over and let her know what he decided. Mary felt her anxiety melting away at his response. To be valued, to be told her thoughts had merit- it was all so novel! Mary left his study with her head spinning.

✳✳✳✳✳

Longbourn was in an uproar when she returned. The instant the carriage pulled into the yard she knew something was different. It was abuzz with activity. There was a wagon already pulled up before the front door and Mrs. Hill was overseeing the unloading of its contents. There was a shocking amount of luggage, considering Mary was unaware they were expecting company.

She alighted from the carriage and approached the hive of activity to inquire of Mrs. Hill as to its source. "We have a guest?"

Mrs. Hill sighed, her face aggrieved. It was a look Mary had not seen in a long time, but she instantly recognized it. "Mrs. Wickham has arrived unexpectedly for an extended visit."

The quantity and sheer mass of luggage attested to the length of her stay. Her heart somewhere around her ankles, Mary asked, "Was there no letter? She did not write?"

Mrs. Hill raised one eyebrow sardonically, which said it all. Mary smiled wryly. "Of course she did not. Lydia would never concern herself with such niceties where they do not affect her."

The housekeeper did not respond to her statement, although Mary had never expected her to. The woman had seen enough during her time in the Bennet household to know all their humiliations. Although she might commiserate with Mary about the return of Lydia, she was too much the professional to express her own opinions to members of the family.

"Has Mr. Wickham come as well?" Mary might as well know the whole of the situation before she was forced to confront it.

"No. He has stayed with his regiment in the North."

Here at least there was reason for some rejoicing. The arrival of her obnoxious and silly sister was an annoyance, but the coming of the man who had been the source of so much pain and humiliation- that was a grievance indeed! She was glad for his absence, recalling all too clearly the crushing blow he had struck to her future. The whole sordid affair might have been patched up with their marriage, but it would never be wholly remedied. Her sisters might all have married and escaped the confines of the small town gossip, but she was still here to hear the whispers and the giggles behind her back.

Mary turned to go in, steeling herself for what awaited her on the other side of the door. She should not have worried. Lydia's exuberance was not for her, except in that she might boast of her married status.

She was greeted with a gladsome cry by her mother. "Look who has come, Mary! Lydia has come! My dear, sweet Lydia!"

Mary obligingly stepped forward to greet her sister with a perfunctory embrace and settled silently into a nearby seat, as she supposed was expected of her.

There was no inquiry as to Mary's first day at Kaverstow; no thought was given to her fatigue. She sat quietly as Lydia expounded on the sorry state of her traveling dress and went into raptures over a piece of ribbon she had espied through a shop window.

At length, the hour for dinner arrived. Mary's stomach grumbled its protest at being ignored for so long, and it was with relief that she sat down to dine. Here at least there was a reprieve; here at least she did not have to sit idly by while her sister monopolized the conversation.

Mary was accustomed to being ignored, but the sudden reappearance of Lydia gave new meaning to the term. At least when her sisters had been at home she could have taken some comfort in their company. There had always been someone else with which to engage in conversation. Now, their mother's attention was focused solely on Lydia, and while Mary might have found a companion in her father, his occasional glances up from his meal never found her gaze.

He might have been enticed from his silence by Lizzy's witty repartee, but Mary could hold no such inducement for him. The hearty meal, at least, gave her some solace, until her sister turned her attention to her halfway through dinner.

"I am sure you must envy me, Mary, for my dear Mr. Wickham. I only hope you may have half my good fortune! You must come visit me this winter. I should think there will be some balls and I will take care to get good partners for you. I daresay I shall get a husband for you before the winter is over!"

"Oh, yes!" their mother cooed. "I shall like that beyond anything! Just think- all five daughters, married!"

Mary laid down her fork. "*I* should think I shall be far too busy this winter teaching the children at Kaverstow to visit you."

Lydia giggled. "La! I forgot! Mamma told me it was so, but I could scarce believe it! Mary Bennet, a governess! *I* should much prefer a husband."

Mary ground her teeth in an effort to check her tongue. She longed to launch into some diatribe on morality, and the virtues of an honest day's work, but knew it would have no effect on her sister.

Lydia did not even seem to notice her silence. "When you have finished at playing governess, you must come to visit! We have the most lovely shops in the North…" She went on, but Mary heard none of it. Shops and ribbons held little charm for her, and she doubted Lydia had any true intention of playing hostess for her.

It was simply a ruse, designed to suggest that she had something Mary did not, and to create jealousy and envy in the heart of one sister for the other. Mary had no use for such childish games.

She would have wished for Lizzy's sharp tongue or Jane's sweet disposition and common sense to handle Lydia and her ploys, but knew even these would have been just as useless as her own moralizing. Lydia was oblivious to anything of which she chose to be insensible, and that included anyone's feelings but her own.

Mary returned to her meal, but found her appetite had waned. She picked absently at the food still arranged on her plate. She interrupted Lydia's monologue to ask, "How long are you to stay?"

She could tell Lydia was annoyed at the interruption by the way her jaw tightened. "Oh! La! I should think at least a month or so. Perhaps even six weeks, if Mamma should be able to stand it!"

Mary persisted in her questions when Lydia would have turned back to speak to their mother. "My dear brother, Wickham, he does not wish you to be home sooner?"

The sarcasm that slipped into her voice at the words, "dear brother," went right over Lydia's head.

"My dear Wickham," said Lydia, placing on hand over her heart and heaving a dramatic sigh. "He is always so considerate. He understands quite how it is between a woman and her Mamma! He would not dream of separating us again so soon! He assured me he would do quite well on his own."

Mary raised one brow at that statement but made no further comment. She was reasonably sure he would do quite well on his own, indeed, without the restraint of a wife to hamper him! And she could well imagine what follies he would engage in while his wife was away. Foolish, foolish Lydia!

She laid down her fork and pushed back from the table, pleading a headache as her excuse. She need not have bothered, she reflected ruefully as she climbed the stairs to her room. No one had paid her any attention anyway as she left the table.

The fire in her room had died down to a glow in the hearth, but she did not take the time to stoke it, despite the chill in the dark room. She quickly readied herself for bed and burrowed under the covers. As the warmth slowly seeped back into her limbs, she sought the comfort of an old friend. A worn copy of Fordyce's Sermons rested on the night stand. She reached out and picked it up, her fingers caressing the smooth leather cover.

She smiled fondly down at it. Lizzy had always held that the views it contained were antiquated and ridiculous, and Mary knew, deep down, that it was true. But the book had given her hope when she had desperately needed it; hope that she too could be desirable as a wife; that someone out there could love her if she comported herself correctly, regardless of the fact that she was plain and unremarkable. It was a life she could only dream of.

But dream she did, the book clasped tightly to her chest. She dreamt of a home of her own, of someone to love that would love her in return. She dreamt of a warm fire in the evenings and animated conversation. She wistfully pictured tow-headed children with chocolate brown eyes, and walks through the gardens, and a library full of books waiting to be read.

Eventually, her thoughts lulled her into sleep, her dreams taking on new dimensions in the confines of her mind and allowing her escape from the harsh reality of her own life.

CHAPTER SIX

Mary was thankful that Lydia was not an early riser as she snuck down the back stairs the next morning. The gray light of dawn only just illuminated the treads of the stairs enough for her to traverse them. She stepped lightly, cautious so as not to wake the sleeping household.

A quick stop in the kitchen nabbed her a leftover crust of bread in her pocket before she was out the back door. She headed out to her favorite little copse of trees to think and prepare for the day ahead of her.

She took a seat on a stump and munched contentedly. She had a little bit of time before she had to be off to Kaverstow. She wondered if Thomas had thought over her suggestions, and what, if any, rules he had come up with. She mentally outlined her lesson plans for the day and reflected fondly on her charges. In the end, she analyzed her feelings and realized she was actually rather looking forward to going to Kaverstow. Society, and Lydia, might look down on her for choosing this path, but it left her active and fulfilled, which she could not find fault with.

She ate the last bite of bread and brushed the crumbs from her fingers. She was not in the habit of such early morning adventures, but she could certainly understand their appeal. Lizzy had been quite fond of them, and by all accounts, still was. They served a useful purpose, giving one time to consider things before being thrust into the day's activities.

She rose and slowly began her journey back to the house. Lydia would still likely be safely ensconced in bed, and her mother rarely sought her out before breakfast. Her father seldom had any use for her whatsoever. She should be able to finish readying herself to depart for Kaverstow unmolested.

When she descended the stairs sometime later to depart, no one outside of the maids had intruded on her solitude. Just as she hesitated on the last step, her mother's voice rang out down the hallway. "Mary! Mary, wait just a moment! I would have a word with you!"

Mary cringed. She had been so close to making it out the door without any interference from her mother. Slowly, she turned to face Mrs. Bennet as the woman scurried down the hall toward her. "Yes, Mamma?"

"You must be sure to invite Mr. Bowen to dine with us."

"But he just dined with us last week!"

"Yes, but we do not want him to lose interest in you! He must come! Besides, Lydia has come now, and I am sure he will want to see your sister after she has been away for so long."

Mary sighed and gave up her attempt to change her mother's mind. "I will ask him, but I cannot guarantee he will accept." *Especially after the fiasco last time he came to dinner,* she added silently. The man would have to be daft to willingly repeat that experience.

Her mother was satisfied with her response. She hurried off happily, calling for Hill to go over the dinner menus for the week.

Mary shook her head in amazement at the gall of the woman and headed out to the carriage, grateful that at least she had been spared Lydia's effusions that morning.

*****

Thomas tried to apply himself to his work, but all his senses were on high alert, straining for any sign of Miss Bennet's arrival. He must have jumped up to look out the window two or three times, thinking he had heard the carriage on the drive, before he actually spied the horses.

His heart rate spiked at the sight. He stayed at the window to watch her alight. As much as he wished to hurry down the stairs to greet her, he held himself back. She would not appreciate him treating her with such preference. He had to let her do her job, without his interference.

She disappeared inside, out of his sight, and he had to be content with that. He seated himself at his desk, aware she would send John to him shortly. He steeled himself for the boy's enthusiasm about the promised day in the fields.

He still flinched when John threw open the door, banging it against the wall, and came bounding in. His nephew flung himself into the chair across from him and bounced in his seat. "Are you ready, Uncle Thomas?"

"Just about, John. If you will sit quietly and let me finish these calculations, we can depart. I have already ordered the horses to be readied for us."

John tried to sit still, Thomas could tell; he really did. But he failed abysmally. The constant creaking as he shifted and the tattoo of his fingers on the wooden arm of the chair distracted Thomas from his task. Finally, he conceded defeat. His calculations would have to wait until they returned. He set aside his papers and ink. "All right. I am ready. Let us go."

His nephew was out of his chair before the words had left his mouth. He chuckled wryly as he followed the ten-year-old out the door and down the steps. If only he could harness the lad's enthusiasm.

He had chosen a gentle pony for the boy's mount, unsure how often John had had the opportunity to practice his riding skills. John scrambled up into the saddle. What he lacked in finesse, he made up for with his zest for the ride.

Thomas turned his attention to his own mount. He was an accomplished rider, having been in the saddle since he was a toddler, but his preferred mount was still a dependable, steady stallion he had owned for several years.

Another man may have preferred a mount with more spirit, that would challenge his abilities, but Thomas preferred to be able to focus on the task at hand, not controlling his horse.

He settled himself in the saddle, giving the stallion an affectionate pat on the neck as the horse shifted under his weight. "Whoa, boy." He glanced over at John, who was perched on the pony, grinning widely. He matched his nephew's boyish grin with his own. "Are you ready?"

John's eager nod was all the encouragement he needed to spur the stallion into motion. He kept them to a sedate trot so the boy could keep up as they headed down the lane and then out across the fields. Thomas was pleased to see that John kept up pretty well as they rode, even navigating a tricky stream crossing with ease.

It was a good twenty minute ride to the fields he had planned on inspecting that morning with his steward. The man was waiting for them on the outskirts of the field, supervising the workers, when they arrived. Thomas was glad he had brought John along, as it was a good learning experience for the boy. The field was not draining properly and had become water-logged. It was a common problem in the spring months, and he and the steward quickly agreed on a plan of action to eliminate the problem.

John watched the interchange with wide eyes. His father was a sailor, and Thomas reflected that he had probably never had the occasion to be party to conversations such as this. The process of farming was completely new to him. Thomas would not discourage the boy from pursuing a career at sea, but he did want to at least make sure John knew he had other options.

His steward immediately moved to implement their plan, instructing the workers while Thomas and John looked on. Thomas took care to explain to John what exactly they were doing to correct the problem, and why what they had decided on was the best plan of action.

His nephew listened intently to everything he said and asked pertinent questions as the discussion continued. Thomas was impressed with the boy's insight, and told him so. John lit up under the praise.

The steward returned, and Thomas stepped back, allowing John to pepper the other man with questions. He looked on with a smile. It was nice to see John so engaged in an activity, to see his pride in being involved in the adult discussion. He had not realized how great a difference a little encouragement could make.

He thought of his sister as he watched John interact with his steward, and felt a twinge of sadness that she was not here to see her son and the young man he was growing into. John reminded him of Anne in so many ways. He had the same stubborn streak Anne had always had that kept him refusing to admit when he was wrong, and the same wide, expressive eyes. He knew she would have been proud to see him, finding his place in the world at Kaverstow. He certainly was.

Thomas refused to allow himself to descend into the melancholy that threatened at the thought of his sister. He needed to keep his energy high and his attitude positive if this excursion was to be a success.

They remained in the field for awhile longer, overseeing the proceedings, before Thomas' steward mentioned another area he would like Thomas to see as well. Part of a fence had been washed away by flooding from the early spring rains and needed repairing. The steward led the way, turning his mount down a seldom-used path. Thomas brought up the rear, keeping John safely sandwiched between them. He did not want the boy to go wandering off and get lost. They were far from his usual haunts, and the seemingly never-ending farmland and tracts of woodland could easily become bewildering, even to someone familiar with the area.

John did not seem to recognize the precautionary measure for what it was, which Thomas was grateful for. Had he realized the purpose of such a move, there was no knowing how he might have reacted. That stubborn streak he had inherited from his mother sometimes manifested itself in fierce independence and an unwillingness to accept assistance. Thomas still had not quite worked out how to overcome that tendency in his nephew.

The bright sunshine that lit the path ahead signaled that they had reached their destination. Thomas frowned at the sight that lay before him. The steward's blithe description had not prepared him for the extent of the damage.

The fence line was now virtually nonexistent. Only a few posts remained, jutting up forlornly out of the silt the swollen river had deposited as it receded. He was fortunate the livestock had all been moved to higher ground before the flooding. The fence would never have contained them in the shape it was in.

Thomas dismounted to inspect the damage more closely, throwing the reins of his mount up to John to hold. The ground was still soft and boggy with water, sucking at his boots as he walked. When he hit the silt, the slippery muck almost caused his feet to slide out from under him.

He glanced up and caught John watching him with something akin to concern. It warmed his heart to see the boy respond in such a way. It was hard to know if any of his sister's children felt any affection for him as their uncle, they had had so little time to build any familial bonds, but maybe he was actually coming to mean something to John. It was nice to think it might be true.

Wrapped up in the warm glow of possibilities, he took a giant step forward… and left his boot behind in the mud. Its sudden absence caught him by surprise and set him off balance. He flailed around precariously, struggling to maintain his balance on the one foot he had planted deep into the muck, while keeping his other stocking-clad foot out of the mud.

He had stilled, poised on the edge of success, when an errant gust of wind sent him toppling over. He tried to catch himself with his hands, but wound up landing heavily on his rear, his arms planted elbow deep in the sludge. He sat there, stunned, for several seconds, before he pried one arm loose from the silt and tried to shake off the mud clinging to his sleeve. He wrinkled his nose with distaste.

John burst out laughing, drawing Thomas' attention up from his own predicament. Even his steward was trying to hide a grin behind his hand. Thomas couldn't stop the small smile that surfaced at the boy's laughter. He glanced down at himself and shook his head at the mess he had created. His valet was going to have an apoplexy when he saw him.

He pried his other arm out of the mud and managed to lever himself into a standing position. Mud slid off his trousers, falling in huge globs off his rear. He took a step forward and cringed at the mud squishing between his toes. Stepping carefully, he retrieved the boot he had lost and traipsed toward the fence. He had come this far and done enough damage that he might as well finish the job he had intended to do. He could hardly make the situation worse.

By the time he made it to the remaining posts, he was knee-deep in muck. But since his clothes were already ruined, he paid it no mind. Instead, he carefully inspected the timber, making a mental checklist of all the work that would have to be done before this piece of land would be usable again.

It was an extensive list.

When he had finished, he turned around and started the laborious trek back to where the other two waited with his mount. John was still smirking, but his steward was watching him closely, respect in his eyes. Thomas gave him a nod back as he collected his horse's reins. The man may have found humor in the situation, but he knew Thomas was serious about his responsibilities, especially when it came to Kaverstow, and he respected him for it. Thomas was no idle master, and he was certainly no fool.

Thomas swung himself into the saddle with his one booted foot, settling his stocking foot into the stirrup. He kept a firm grip on his other boot with one hand. His clothes might be ruined, but the mud could be wiped off his leather boots as long as he kept any from getting inside them.

He turned his mount towards the path, taking the lead. "I think we had better head back to the house. This fence will require extensive repairs and I should like to get started on the preparations right away." He grinned wryly. "And I think a change of clothes is in order, as well."

"As you say, sir." His steward followed his lead, leaving room for John to ride between them.

John seemed disappointed as he took his place. He pouted. "Do we have to go back? Surely, there are other fields we could visit."

Thomas looked back over his shoulder and said firmly, "Sometimes being a landowner means setting priorities. This fence needs to be fixed so we have fresh fields for the cattle to graze in this summer. That has to take priority over the other fields, which do not need my attention at this time. Mr. Jones is perfectly capable of overseeing them without our interference. Besides, I think you have had enough excitement for one day."

Thomas could tell the boy wanted to protest further, but he wisely held his tongue. Thomas turned back in his saddle and shifted his focus to getting back to the house. Being on horseback had made him suddenly conscious that he had mud in some very uncomfortable places.

*****

Mary paced by the windows as the girls worked on their samplers. She chewed on her bottom lip, fretting over delivering the dreaded dinner invitation. She had not seen Mr. Bowen all morning. Sophia and Emilia had been quick to inform her upon her arrival that he was taking John with him into the fields today. She could only imagine how excited their brother must be for the opportunity, but that had left her with no chance to convey her mother's message.

She picked absently at a loose thread on her sleeve. Her mother would not be happy if she neglected to invite Mr. Bowen to dinner. She sighed. But then again, when had she ever been able to make her mother happy?

The bright sunlight streaming through the window beckoned to her, the invitation difficult for her distracted mind to resist. She did not even try. Turning to the girls, who were bent diligently over their samplers, she asked, "Shall we take a turn about the garden?"

The suggestion was eagerly taken up. Mary wrapped them up snuggly against any chill that might remain in the spring air and ushered them down the stairs and out the door.

She paused outside the door in shock as the oddest spectacle met her eyes. The girls giggled behind her at the sight and Mary fought to maintain her composure.

The gentleman had apparently just returned, as the grooms were leading their mounts away. Thomas limped forward, his gait uneven with only the one boot on, and bowed awkwardly to Mary. "Miss Bennet."

He cringed as her gaze ran the full length of him and returned to his face, her eyes dancing. She caught her lip beneath her teeth, but Thomas could still see the smile she was attempting to hide.

"Mr. Bowen," she said smoothly. "I hope your ride was productive."

The splatters of drying mud on his face and arms were beginning to itch. He shifted uncomfortably, trying not to be rude. "It was informative. There is always much to do about the property." He ran a hand through his hair and Mary jumped back to avoid the glob of black muck that fell free at the movement. Thomas flushed bright red. "If you will excuse me, Miss Bennet, I must change. Please see to John until I return." He gathered what shards of his dignity remained and marched into the house, his back ramrod straight until he was out of her sight. Then he sprinted up the stairs to the tub that awaited him.

Mary absently noted the muddy footprints that followed him inside and wondered how the maids would ever get them out of the carpets.

John sauntered up to them and the girls were eager to ply him with questions about his morning.

"Where did you go, John?" Sophia asked.

He rocked back on his heels and regarded them coolly, his nose in the air. "We *men* had *work* to do."

Mary raised one eyebrow at his attitude and Sophia recoiled from his haughty demeanor. "Well, then, don't tell me," she pouted. "*We women* are going for a turn about the garden." She whirled about and stomped off, her chin raised determinedly.

Emilia eyed her brother seriously. "I think you are being mean," she told him bluntly, and followed her sister down the path.

Mary could see the boy's attitude wilt before her eyes, but he stubbornly refused to react to his sisters' rebuff. She smiled at him. "Come along, John. Your uncle will join us when he has changed."

She laid one gentle hand on his back and guided him on to the path. Mary was content to let the girls run ahead, keeping one eye on them. There would be no repeat of the day before if she had anything to do with it.

*****

Thomas' valet had met him in his chambers with unabashed horror, sending a surge of guilt through him. He could tell the man was grieved at the damage he had done to his appearance and the state of his attire. There was nothing that could be done; the clothing would have to be discarded. But his valet had clutched the dirty boots to his chest with relief.

It was almost comical, the man's reaction, but Thomas was glad to know the man took such pride in his work. He shed the clothes that were stiff with mud and sank eagerly into the warm water his valet had prepared. He rested his head against the rim of the tub and groaned.

Mary Bennet must think him a bumbling fool.

He had never appeared to such disadvantage before in front of a young lady. Even his disastrous social excursions had never found him in such a state.

He ducked his head under the water and tried to scrub the mud out of his hair. The water quickly turned brown with his efforts. Miss Bennet's appalled reaction to the mud falling from his hair replayed against his closed eyelids. But even worse was the smile that had hovered about her mouth.

He was never going to live this down. There had been too many witnesses. He was just going to have to find the humor in the situation and do his best to let it roll off his back. He had to admit, he *had* been a sight. While he had never actually gotten a good look at himself in the mirror before his valet had hustled him into his dressing room, he could tell just by the reactions of everyone around him that it hadn't been pretty.

He resurfaced and reached for a towel to wipe the water from his eyes. He quickly scrubbed the mud from his limbs and climbed out of the tub. Miss Bennet would be waiting for him to reclaim John and he was eager to replace the tainted memory of him in her mind with a more favorable one.

He allowed his valet to fuss over him, brushing his coat and tying his cravat into the sophisticated Oriental style. He surveyed his reflection in the mirror with approval when the man had finished. He hoped Miss Bennet would appreciate his efforts.

His valet finally stepped back, announcing he was finished, and Thomas was free to go down. He paused just inside the door to tug at his waistcoat and straighten his jacket. He resisted the urge to run a finger under his collar and took a deep breath to calm his nerves.

He did not know why he was so nervous. He had no reason to be. Mary Bennet was his employee. She did not think of him as a prospective suitor, like her mother might. His clothes and manners should mean little to her. Yet, he could not seem to help desiring her good opinion. She gave it so parsimoniously, it would be an honor to earn it.

He rested his hand on the door knob, lost in thought. Mary Bennet might be his governess, but she was like no other woman he had ever met. She was quiet and solicitous. She listened attentively when he spoke and gave her opinion decidedly, but without malice. She respected him, when so many of the Ton found him ridiculous.

She was not afraid to be different. In fact, was he not her employer, he might be tempted…

A discreet cough from behind him interrupted his thoughts. His butler, Bertram, stood there, watching him bemusedly. Thomas flushed scarlet under his scrutiny as he realized how he must look, standing there with his hand on the knob. He gave the man a stiff nod and pushed the door open, exiting quickly.

Once outside, the bright sunlight lifted his spirits and he pushed any lingering self-doubts to the back of his mind. He was determined to enjoy what little time he could spend outside with Miss Bennet and the children before his study beckoned.

It was not difficult to find them. They had not strayed too far into the gardens, preferring the more open spaces for their games. The children were engaged in racing across the grass while Miss Bennet looked on. Thomas went to join her.

"I hope they have been behaving for you, Miss Bennet," Thomas said.

She looked over at him with a welcoming smile. "Very much so, Mr. Bowen. I have been endeavoring to keep watch over them so there will be no repeat of yesterday, but it appears there is no thought of that."

"I am glad to hear it."

They fell silent and Mary hazarded a glance at the man beside her from under her lashes. This was her opportunity to speak to him, but she felt herself hesitating, now that the moment was upon her. How would he react? Would he think her too forward?

She steeled herself for a negative answer. "My mother has requested that I invite you to dinner tonight, Mr. Bowen." She waited anxiously for his response, her shoulders tense, her gaze ostensibly on the children frolicking before them.

Thomas was silent for several minutes as he contemplated how to respond. His last meal at the Bennet's had been uncomfortable, and he was sure Mrs. Bennet had only renewed the invitation with one purpose in mind.

He snuck a glance at Miss Bennet and noted her stiff back and neck. She was trying desperately to appear like his answer did not matter to her, but it did. He did not know why it should. She could have no designs upon his person. Perhaps it was her mother's displeasure she feared. Regardless, he could not bring himself to tell her no and see those shoulders sag under her disappointment.

He turned his gaze back to the children. "I have no other engagement. I shall be delighted to attend."

Her relief was palpable, although she did her best not to let it show. "I shall tell her to expect you then."

Thomas smiled a little, happy to have pleased her, and let the silence lengthen between them. It was a comfortable silence. They were each acutely aware of the other's presence and any slight motion on the other's part was noticed. But the children's presence was a necessary excuse, allowing them the privilege of the other's company.

After quite a while, being reluctant to part, Mary called the girls to her and gathered them up to return inside. John, too, recognized that the time for play was over, and came to stand by his uncle's side as Mary led the girls back to the schoolroom.

"What are we going to do this afternoon?" John asked.

Thomas watched the girls go before turning his attention to the boy at his side. "I have some letters to write about mending that fence, and you, young man, have some figures to calculate." He clapped one hand affectionately against the boy's shoulder and steered him in the direction of the door.

John grumbled good-naturedly under his breath, but he went willingly. Thomas smiled. They were finally making progress. Now if he could just figure out discipline.

CHAPTER SEVEN

Thomas fidgeted under the expert hand of his valet as he dressed him for dinner that night at Longbourn. He felt as trussed up as the turkey that would surely grace the table at dinner. He just hoped Mrs. Bennet would not put *him* on a platter as well! He shifted uncomfortably as the man brushed invisible dust from his shoulders. His clothing might start out as impeccable, but he doubted it would last the night in that condition. He was already itching to loosen his cravat.

He stifled the impulse to run a hand through his hair. His valet had spent well over twenty minutes styling his blonde locks into perfect submission and he would not insult the man by messing up all his hard work. Not to mention it would just mean he would have to spend another twenty minutes in front of the mirror. And he was already running behind as it was.

He had underestimated how long it would take to complete his letters with John nagging him every five minutes for help with his sums. The dinner bell had already sounded by the time he had sent the boy up to join his sisters in the nursery. It had taken him an additional ten minutes to finish his correspondence before he could go upstairs himself to change.

His valet stepped back to give him one last once-over before he gave his master a nod of approval. Thomas was relieved as the man excused himself, but one glance at the watch at his waist erased that. He rushed down the stairs and into the carriage. He was already late. But if he hurried, he might be able to catch the Bennets before they went in to dine.

He only hoped Miss Mary Bennet was not too disappointed by his late arrival.

*****

"Oh, my poor nerves! Such flutterings and tremblings, all over me! I cannot bear the thought of such ill-usage by one of our neighbors!" Mrs. Bennet fell back against the sofa, one hand flung dramatically against her forehead.

Mary looked up from the book she had been hoping to lose herself in and said, "Mr. Bowen is a busy man, Mamma. I hardly think being a few minutes late warrants such a label."

"*I* think it is quite fashionable to be one of the last to arrive," Lydia chimed in with a giggle. "Then all eyes are on you when you do come in. La! What fun!"

"I do not think a dinner party with the family can be considered a fashionable engagement. We hardly stand on ceremony here," Mary retorted. "Anyways, Mr. Bowen is not the sort of man who would delay his hosts for such a trivial reason as that!"

Mrs. Bennet sniffed. "Well, I certainly do not know when I have been so ill-used in my own household. But we shall give him a few minutes more before we go in, just in case he should have come to some accident along the way."

Mr. Bennet looked up from his own reading material. "I am surprised at your sensibilities, my dear Mrs. Bennet. Should he have indeed come to an accident, it will be a comfort to know that it was in the pursuit of one of your daughters."

The reminder of a possible suitor for the last of her unmarried daughters brought a smile to Mrs. Bennet's face. "Five daughters married! Lady Lucas will be positively green with envy, for she has three still at home!"

Mary hurried to interrupt this line of thought before it could grow out of hand. "Mr. Bowen is my employer, Mamma, not my suitor. I would thank you to remember that."

Mrs. Bennet waved away such concerns. "Oh, shush with you! Mr. Bowen would do very well as a husband for you. You must help him on and encourage him!"

Lydia giggled. "You cannot expect her to attract Mr. Bowen looking like that."

Mrs. Bennet took a good look at Mary and said, "Your sister is right; you look far too pale, Mary. That will not do! Here, let us put a little color in your cheeks!" She advanced on Mary, fingers eagerly outstretched.

Mary tried to evade the fingers intent on pinching color into her cheeks and failed. "Ow! Mamma! Stop that! Pappa! Tell her to stop!"

Mr. Bennet looked on without the slightest inclination to interfere with his wife's machinations. "I sympathize with your motives, Mary, but you must find your comfort in knowing that your Mamma has only your best interests at heart. She will not be content until she has seen all five of her daughters married."

Mary scowled at this speech and, when her mother had finished with her, put up her book to block any further assaults upon her person.

At length, it was determined they could wait no longer, and they had all risen to go out into the hall when Mrs. Hill appeared at the door and announced their guest.

"Mr. Bowen!" Mrs. Bennet gushed. "It is so good of you to join us! I do hope the roads were to your satisfaction?"

Thomas bowed. "They were very well, thank you. I hope you will accept my apologies for my tardiness. There were some pressing matters of business I had to attend to that set me quite behind for the evening."

"Nonsense!" Mr. Bennet harrumphed. "There is no need for an apology. We had quite given you up in an accident!"

Thomas was startled by this pronouncement and, unsure how to respond, he stood there in silence for several moments before Lydia broke in, saying, "La! I do hope we can go in now that you have come. I am starving!"

"You use the word too callously, Lydia," Mary bit out, annoyed with her lack of decorum. "I doubt you have ever been truly starving."

"Indeed," Thomas added awkwardly, eager to back her up. "The word comes originally from the Old English *steorfan,* which means to die. And since you seem a stout, well-grown girl, I am disinclined to believe you mean to use the word so."

All four of his hosts turned their gazes upon him to stare in shock at such a speech. Thomas shifted uncomfortably under their scrutiny, mentally reprimanding himself. *I cannot believe I did it again!*

Then Lydia burst out laughing. "La! How droll you all sound!"

Mary and Thomas exchanged glances and Mary sighed. Lydia was incorrigible. "Let us go in," she said. There was no sense standing around debating how hungry they were when they could be eating.

They settled around the table, Mr. Bennet at the head, with Lydia and Mary on one side and Mrs. Bennet and Thomas on the other. When the first course had been laid out before them and the servants had gone, Mrs. Bennet turned her attention to her favorite activity- matchmaking.

"So, Mr. Bowen, you must be quite pleased to have my Mary in your household. She is so very sensible."

Thomas looked up from his spoonful of white soup to smile at Mary. "I assure you, Miss Bennet's assistance is greatly appreciated."

Mary blushed under his scrutiny and returned his smile with a tentative one of her own. "Truly, it is my pleasure. I enjoy spending time with the children."

Mrs. Bennet smiled broadly at their interaction. "I did not always have such high hopes for Mary. She is so very plain, you know-"

The smile fled from Mary's face as she cut off her mother, horrified. "Mamma!"

Thomas lowered his gaze to his meal and shifted in his seat at the sudden tension in the room.

Mrs. Bennet looked bewildered. "It is the truth! Why should I not tell the truth? Everyone knows it to be so!" She looked around the room, seeking reassurance.

Lydia was blissfully unaware of any discord. "Oh, Mamma! You know Mary does not like to hear her faults advertised so publicly. Besides, it is not her fault she is so very plain, nor very tall."

Mary hung her head, cheeks flaming with embarrassment. Thomas snuck a glance at her, feeling acutely her shame and humiliation.

Mr. Bennet finally decided it was time to lead the discussion in a more fruitful direction. "Neither Mary's countenance nor her height can have any effect on her position as governess. I am glad to know she is fulfilling her duties in your household so well, Mr. Bowen, especially in so short a time of actual employment."

Thomas cleared his throat. "Yes, well, I can already see a great deal of improvement in my nephew and nieces' comportment." *It was true*, he tried to convince himself. He had not had any problems with Sophia or Emilia while Mary had been there to oversee them. It was only after she was gone for the day that he had caught them trying to create a rope swing off the balcony. Now *that* had been a close call. How did one go about making rules for children when you never knew what they would do next?

"If I should have any children, they shall not have half as much fun as I have," Lydia bragged. "And although they will no doubt be very beautiful (for my dear Mr. Wickham is very handsome and I am no less) I shall outshine them all."

"I should think if you do have children, it will mean a great deal *less* fun for you," Mary commented with a superior sniff.

Lydia ignored her. "La! What fun it will be to go to all the parties and dances when they come out! I shall introduce my daughters to all the officers!" She giggled.

Mr. Bennet raised an eyebrow. "While I cannot share your enthusiasm for a red coat, I rather hope any granddaughters of mine will be spared your method for getting a husband. Although there can be no hope, I am sure, of them showing any sort of sense."

"What good is sense," said Lydia, "When there are gowns and fans and balls to be had! I would much prefer a husband to good sense!"

Mary barely restrained herself from rolling her eyes, but Mrs. Bennet chimed in with her approval. "She is quite right, my dear Mr. Bennet! What good does sense do a girl without a husband to protect and provide for her? She had much rather be beautiful, I daresay."

Mr. Bennet steepled his hands before him. "Yes, my dear, I quite expected you to say such a thing." He looked wistful.

"It has been almost three years since I have heard any sense in this house. Not since my Lizzy left me."

Thomas squirmed in his seat. Would this conversation never resume a normal tangent? He had heard Mary Bennet insulted at every turn by every member of her family, yet he could not see the truth in their words. He turned his gaze to the young lady. She was certainly not plain, and while she was on the petite side, he thought her height rather perfect, since the top of her head was about even with his chin. *The perfect height to kiss her easily,* he thought.

His errant thoughts startled him and he shook his head to dispel them. Where had that thought come from? He had no business thinking of kissing Mary Bennet. The woman was in his employ for goodness' sakes!

His gaze dropped to linger on her mouth.

But she did have the prettiest rosy, bow-shaped lips- his imagination threatened to run away with him still. He gave his head another shake to rid it of the persistent images and forced his eyes back on his own plate.

He firmly turned his thoughts to the last and most perplexing of the accusations laid against her. Mr. Bennet had commented on a lack of good sense. How could that be so with Mary still in the household? She had demonstrated remarkable perception and wisdom in every one of their conversations. Her suggestions were always logical and well thought out. It was most puzzling, indeed.

The conversation had continued on around him. He was recalled to it by Lydia asking him, "Do you not think so, Mr. Bowen?" She batted her eyelashes coquettishly at him.

Thomas was confused by the maneuver. "I beg your pardon, Mrs. Wickham; do you have something in your eye?"

Lydia scowled at his misunderstanding. "No, of course not. Do not be silly, Mr. Bowen."

This only served to confuse Thomas more. "Oh. Well, in that case, you will have to remind me of your question, Mrs. Wickham. I am afraid I was not attending to the conversation."

Lydia did so, happily. "I asked if you did not think that a lively nature was most desirable in a wife?"

Thomas paused, aware he needed to word his reply carefully. She was up to some mischief, though he could not fully understand what. He suspected it might have to do with Mary, and making herself appear to better advantage than her sister. The liveliness of the one, although shown to her advantage in private, could be nothing when in the company of the other.

Finally, he said reluctantly, "I am certain there are many gentlemen who would feel that way."

Lydia took this as a confirmation, but only Mrs. Bennet made that mistake as well. Mary shot him a grateful look, while Mr. Bennet raised one brow in surprise. The older man nodded thoughtfully, just a hint of respect in his eyes.

They all laid down their utensils as the servants came in to remove the first course and lay out the next. They sat silently, Lydia fidgeting in her seat, until the servants had all filed out once again.

Thomas jumped at the chance to change the subject to something more suitable. "The militia is to continue in town, I hear. There had been some talk of their removal."

This statement, intended as it had been for Mr. Bennet, had the effect of sending Mrs. Bennet and Mrs. Wickham into raptures. Thomas was quite startled by the result of his words on the ladies and turned a bewildered gaze on Mary. She shrugged.

"Should I call for the smelling salts, my dear Mrs. Bennet?" Mr. Bennet commented drolly. "Or shall the hysterics be of short duration?"

Mrs. Bennet waved him away. "Oh, my dear Mr. Bennet! You cannot know the good the sight of a red coat does to my nerves! To know we are so well-protected-! I would scarce know how we would get on without them in the village. It is too much to think of their removal! Too much!"

"Your vehemence does you justice," Mr. Bennet replied. "But I think you have rather frightened Mr. Bowen with it. You had much better speak of something less taxing on your poor nerves."

"Very well." Mrs. Bennet sniffed. "But you must own that it is a comfort to know there are men like Lydia's own Mr. Wickham nearby to protect us!"

"Yes, that is a comfort indeed."

Thomas wondered at the bitter cynicism that traced through his words. Mr. Bennet had always had a sarcastic streak, but this- this was something more, something deeper than mere sarcasm. What history did the man have with Mr. Wickham to warrant such a tone?

Thomas remembered very little of the charming Mr. Wickham from his time in Meryton. He had been too wrapped up in the running of Kaverstow to pay much attention to the local gossip. He had gathered that Lydia's marriage had been somewhat of a rushed affair, but perhaps there was more to the story than he had realized.

But this was neither the time nor the place to pry into private family affairs, so instead he endeavored to shift the topic yet again, hopeful of his eventual success. He searched his mind for a topic suitable with the ladies' present and smiled when he came up with one that would do quite nicely.

"Did you hear that Mrs. Long's niece is to be married?"

While the Bennets had, indeed, heard such news, the interjections and exclamations that such a topic merited were enough to see them through the third course and into the separation of the sexes.

After the ladies had left the room, Mr. Bennet rose to pour the port. He opened the decanter and poured them each a glass, his back to Thomas. "You are either a very brave man or a very stupid one to return for a family dinner again so soon." He turned back to the table and handed Thomas his glass before taking his seat. "I cannot decide which. Tell me, Mr. Bowen, have you some sort of mental illness that inclines you towards masochism?"

Thomas took a sip of his drink, using the maneuver to buy time to decide on his response. Mr. Bennet studied him closely, looking for what, he knew not. The older man's eyes were shrewd, his countenance deceptively open. Thomas knew he was being tested.

He swirled the liquid in his glass and swallowed, letting the alcohol burn its way down the back of his throat. "Perhaps you can tell me, sir, as it appears to me you practice it yourself, by living in this household."

Mr. Bennet let out a bark of laughter at his response. "Well said, Mr. Bowen. I will own that I find some enjoyment in the ridiculousness of my wife and daughters. They are good for some amusement at least."

"It appears to me that you find great amusement in allowing your daughters to be belittled in front of your guests."

"They do that to themselves, I fear."

"Mrs. Wickham, perhaps, but not Miss Bennet. You can find no fault in her decorum. Indeed, in all my dealings with her, I have found her deserving of the utmost respect."

Mr. Bennet cocked his head and raised a brow. "You speak very decidedly for one so young and for one who claims no attachment to my daughter. Do you speak as an admirer, Mr. Bowen, or as an employer?"

Thomas flushed, Mr. Bennet's query the source of quandary and confusion for him. He did not know where this determination to defend Mary Bennet arose from. He did admire her, greatly, but he was not about to be caught in her mother's clutches by admitting that to her father. "As an employer, of course."

Mr. Bennet did not press him further on the subject, although Thomas could tell the man found his answer to be a source of great amusement.

"I grant you, Mr. Bowen, that I may not always treat my children with the respect they deserve. Mary has never given me cause to fear for the family virtue. Her indiscretions are minor compared to the failings of her sisters. She has always acted with the utmost sensibility, even to a fault sometimes."

"No person can be without faults, Mr. Bennet. We all have our foibles. Even you, I daresay."

Mr. Bennet laughed. "You are quite right, my dear lad." He set down his empty glass. "I think we have left the ladies to themselves for sufficiently long enough. Shall we join them?"

Thomas inclined his head. "As you wish, Mr. Bennet." He rose and followed the other man into the hallway, setting his half-full glass on the sideboard as he passed.

They entered the parlor to find the ladies engaged in their own pursuits. Mary had taken up her book again, eager to place it as a barrier between herself and the ignorant musings of her mother and sister. Lydia was standing idly by the fire, fiddling aimlessly with the ribbon under her bust while she chatted with her mother. Mrs. Bennet had seated herself to her full advantage, within easy speaking distance of her favorite daughter, while still with a full view of the door.

She immediately rose upon their entrance, smiling and flapping needlessly as they arranged themselves among the ladies. Tea was soon called for, brought, and poured all around.

Mary laid aside her book to help with the pouring, and was rewarded when Thomas came to collect his own cup. She looked up at him from under the fringe of her lashes. "I hope our little family party has not been too tiresome for you, Mr. Bowen."

Thomas smiled down at her. "Of course not, Miss Bennet. I have found myself experiencing a myriad of emotions tonight, but I assure you that weariness is not one of them."

"I am glad to know that." She handed him his cup and had to be content with that, as her mother's flighty dialogue allowed them no other opportunity for private conversation that night.

At length, Lydia grew bored of listening to her mother talk. She stood to roam the room aimlessly, seeking a distraction. She turned excitedly when her eyes lit upon the pianoforte and an idea presented itself to her. She interrupted the conversation to suggest excitedly, "Let us dance, Mr. Bowen! Mary, you will play for us, won't you?"

She advanced on Thomas before he realized what she was up to, and, seizing him by the hand, pulled him with her to a small section of the room that was clear enough for the sport.

Mary contemplated refusing her sister, especially upon seeing Thomas' panic at being so rudely commandeered, but when he made no protest to the amusement, she acquiesced.

She seated herself at the instrument and arranged the music in front of her.

"Play something lively, Mary! None of those dirges you normally play," Lydia commanded. She looked at her partner and whispered loudly in an aside, "You would think she would realize no one enjoys them."

Thomas forced a pained smile on to his face.

Mary obediently began to pick out a jaunty tune on the instrument and watched as Thomas and Lydia danced, the one with considerably more enthusiasm than the other.

Mary regarded them enviously as she was forced to watch them whirling about. She wished she could be the one standing up with Thomas, even if it was only for a dance in her parents' parlor. She was not the lively, vivacious partner that Lydia was, but she still enjoyed dancing.

"What a charming amusement for young people this is, Mr. Bennet!" Mrs. Bennet observed to her husband with a sigh. "There is nothing like dancing after all. I consider it as one of the first refinements of polished societies."

"Certainly, my dear; and it has the advantage also of being in vogue amongst the less polished societies of the world. Every savage can dance," Mr. Bennet remarked.

Mrs. Bennet paid him little heed. "I receive no inconsiderable pleasure from the sight of my Lydia dancing! Oh how well she looks!"

"It is perhaps the greatest of her accomplishments," Mr. Bennet stated. "Allowing for her talent in securing husbands and avoiding scandal in the process."

The couple kept her at the pianoforte for several sets, only giving her a reprieve when Thomas bowed out, claiming the late hour. He made his excuses, complimenting Mrs. Bennet on the fine meal, and thanking his hosts for an enjoyable evening. His gaze lingered on Mary for a fraction longer than necessary, but he did no more than express his hope of seeing her in the morning.

He collected his coat and hat and was out the door and into his carriage before she knew it. As the door shut behind him, Mary sank into her seat, a sense of profound disappointment lingering in her heart. Why she should be disappointed, she knew not.

"Well, he was a jolly good sport, was he not?" Lydia giggled. "I do not know when I have had such fun during an evening at home. I do hope he will come again."

"I should not doubt it," Mr. Bennet proclaimed. "The man is, after all, one of the neighbors. He cannot always refuse our invitations, even if he had an inclination to."

"How silly you are, Mr. Bennet!" Mrs. Bennet laughed. "As if Mr. Bowen would be inclined to refuse our dinner invitations!"

Mr. Bennet did not reply, only raising an eyebrow at her speech, a sardonic glimmer in his eyes. Mary recognized the look and shared his opinion. Thomas Bowen was far more likely to be disinclined to accept their invitation than he was to accept it. Except- he had appeared to enjoy dancing with Lydia so. Mary tried to quench the spark of jealousy that lit in her breast. What business did she have being envious of Lydia? Her sister was married, for goodness' sakes! It was not as if anything could come of it, despite Lydia's tendency towards flirtation.

She shifted uncomfortably in her seat as Lydia and her mother rehashed the evening around her. If only Lydia had not come! Then she would not be forced to endure such disquieting thoughts.

She excused herself, claiming a headache that was becoming quite real, and retired for the night, eager to leave her interfering relatives behind for the sanctuary of her own room.

CHAPTER EIGHT

A few days later, three little faces peered eagerly at the drive from the nursery window.

"Is she coming today?" asked Sophia.

"I think so," said Emilia. "Uncle Thomas did not say she wasn't."

"She is awful late," said Sophia worriedly. "I hope she has not got into an accident!"

"You girls!" John scoffed. "She probably just left late, like Uncle Thomas does all the time."

"Or maybe her carriage got stuck on the muddy roads," Emilia suggested. "It has been raining all week. Even Uncle Thomas said the roads were near impassable."

"I hope she comes," said Sophia quietly. "I like Miss Bennet. She doesn't yell or say mean things, even when I get my thread all tangled in knots and have to cut it out again. And she kisses my finger when I stab it with my needle." She held up one bandaged forefinger as proof. "It doesn't hurt near as bad when she kisses it better."

John snorted at her childish reasoning but did not correct her. He knew his little sister was still struggling with the loss of their mother, just as they all were, and he could tell that Miss Bennet was helping to fill that void. She would never replace his mother to *him,* but little girls needed a woman to look up to.

Emilia patted her sister on the shoulder. "I like her, too. She is ever so good at playing the pianoforte, even if she does like to play those horridly long concertos."

The squeak of the nursery door on its hinges drew all three of their attentions. They looked over their shoulders as the nurse came in, carrying Helene. "What are you three doing, lined up at the window?" she asked.

"We're watching for Miss Bennet," Sophia supplied helpfully. "She is ever so late."

The nurse shook her head. "You little dears. Miss Bennet will not be around today, for it is Saturday. She has the day off, and Sunday, too."

"Oh," all three chorused. They turned from the window dejectedly.

The nurse bounced Helene on her hip, eliciting a giggle, and tried to encourage them. "Cheer up now! She'll be back again on Monday."

"Yes, Nurse," Sophia said obediently. They filed out of the room, leaving the nurse to stare after them amusedly, still shaking her head.

They made their way out to the gardens, where the girls commandeered a bench to sit on while John kicked idly at a clod of dirt.

"What are we going to do now?" Emilia complained, swinging her feet under her from her perch on the bench. "Uncle Thomas is locked up in his study with Bertram."

John shrugged. "Whatever we want to, I guess."

"I know!" exclaimed Sophia. "Uncle Thomas said that one of the hounds had a litter of pups. We should go to the stables and play with them!"

Emilia agreed enthusiastically and clapped her hands. "Yes. Let's!"

John shrugged again, not wanting to appear too excited about the possibility. "I guess that sounds all right."

They traipsed down the path to the stables, asking one of the grooms for directions to the puppies. If he found it odd to see the children in the stables on their own, he gave no sign of thinking them out of place.

The little girls squealed as they caught sight of the mother dog and her puppies and knelt down so they could reach over the pen and pet the little bundles of fur.

"They are so cute!" Sophia cooed. "Oh, I like that little one with the white spot the best!"

Even John allowed himself to be coerced into picking up one of the puppies so the girls could see it better. They giggled as the squirming dog tried to lick their fingers and faces while they petted it.

"He's so sweet!" Emilia remarked. "I wish we could take him inside so he could sleep with us. The poor thing must be so cold out here in the stables at night."

"Yeah," Sophia chimed in. "Do you think we can take him inside with us, John? Surely Uncle Thomas would not mind. He won't be any trouble."

Their brother shrugged. "I do not see why not. But you will have to be careful to keep him quiet and out of the way so he doesn't bother Uncle Thomas or any of the servants. If they find out they'll make you put him back outside for sure!"

His sisters cheered. "This is going to be so much fun!" Emilia said, rubbing the little dog's ears. "What should we name him?"

"How about Spot?" suggested Sophia.

John nixed that. "No, that is too boring. Everybody names their dog Spot."

"Well, what is his mama's name?" asked Emilia.

John frowned and tried to recall. "I think her name is Dash."

Emilia pondered for a moment. "How about Scamper then?"

"No, I don't like that," Sophia said. "It's too long."

"What about Duke?" suggested John. "That is not too long, and it starts with a 'D' like his mama's name."

The puppy yipped and the girls giggled.

"I think he likes it," Sophia said, and Emilia agreed.

"All right then," John said. "Duke it is."

They fawned over the puppy for a little while longer before Duke squirmed to be let down to play with his brothers and sisters. They watched him for awhile longer, hashing out the details of their plan.

It was agreed that Sophia would find some nice, soft blankets for his bed, while Emilia and John would sneak the puppy inside and find a suitable hiding place to keep him. They would scrounge food for him from their own dinner taken in the nursery.

When they had everything covered, Sophia gave Duke one last scratch on the back before running ahead to see to her part of the plan. Emilia and John lingered awhile longer, cooing over the puppies until there was no one around to see them sneak Duke out.

John tucked the puppy inside his jacket, cupping him tightly against his chest. Emilia led the way inside so she could head off any trouble, lest they run into anyone along the way.

She need not have worried. They did not encounter anyone as they traipsed back through the house and climbed the stairs to the nursery, their muddy footprints leaving a trail behind them.

When they arrived in the nursery, Sophia was waiting for them, her arms full of bedding for the puppy.

Emilia eyed the mound of white cloth overflowing from her arms. "Where did you get that?"

"I could not find any blankets, so I got these out of Uncle Thomas' wardrobe. He's got gobs of them in there, so he should not miss these."

Emilia shrugged. "I think they will work, so long as he does not miss them." She looked around the room. "Now, where shall we keep him?"

"It has to be somewhere Nurse will not look," John stated firmly. "She cannot know we have him up here or she will throw him out for sure."

They pondered this dilemma seriously for quite awhile before they lit upon a solution. The wardrobe was too risky, as Nurse set out their clothes for them in the morning. They discussed and discarded several other options before deciding upon the toy chest set in one corner of the room.

Sophia happily went about preparing a bed for Duke and they settled him into it, propping up the lid a little on the chest so he would have fresh air. Yawning, Duke curled up in his bed and quickly fell asleep, exhausted by his lengthy play time.

Sophia giggled from where they knelt beside the chest, watching him as he kicked in his sleep. "Goodnight Duke."

*****

Mary Bennet left Longbourn early Monday morning in order to cover the distance to Kaverstow on foot, the horses being unavailable to convey her. She hurried, worried that she would be late despite her early departure. It was the first time she had traversed the distance by foot, and she was unsure how long it would take her to make the journey. She had no desire to inconvenience her employer by arriving late. Besides, she was rather looking forward to being with the children again, especially after a trying weekend spent in the company of her mother and Lydia.

The roads were slick with mud and studded with puddles from a spring storm the night before. Twice she almost slipped but caught herself just in time. She tried to hold up her skirts out of the mud but the damage was done. By the time she arrived, her petticoat was six inches deep in mud.

She worried her bottom lip as she carefully cleaned her shoes before going inside. What would Mr. Bowen think of her, showing up in such a state? She snuck up the back stairs, hoping to avoid him until she was more presentable.

By the time she arrived in the nursery, John had already departed to join his uncle and the girls were waiting for her. She got right to work, setting them down with some watercolors and teaching them the correct way to hold the brushes. She watched them carefully as they painted, ensuring they used the correct form. Their first efforts were clumsy at best, but Mary was pleased by the pains they took to follow her instructions.

She was helping Sophia to adjust her grip on the brush when a scratching noise from the corner drew her attention. She looked up and cast her gaze about the room, trying to find the source of the noise. "What was that?"

Emilia glanced up in alarm and then quickly shifted in her seat. "Oh, it was probably just my petticoats rustling."

Mary shook her head. "No, it was something else. It sounded like it was coming from the corner."

"Maybe it was a mouse," suggested Sophia.

"I guess that is possible," mused Mary.

The girls exchanged relieved glances, but then the scratching was replaced by a low whining. They froze in their seats and looked guiltily at Mary.

Mary arched a brow. "I do not think that a mouse would make *that* noise." She listened a moment longer, then started towards the toy chest, following the sound.

She sent the girls a questioning glance when she noticed the lid to the toy chest was ajar, and then bent to open it. The girls held their breath as she lifted the lid and frenzied yipping broke out.

Mary stared down in disbelief at the puppy wagging his tail excitedly at the sight of her. His whole rear end moved with the motion, setting him off balance and sending him wiggling all over the place. Several minutes passed as she silently tried to decide what she should do, the yipping growing in intensity the longer she stood there.

The girls could stand her silence no longer. They nearly tripped over themselves as they raced to join her at the toy chest and explain. Their words tumbled over each other, jumbled and mismatched in their hurry.

"Isn't he cute? His name is Duke," Sophia said. "He has been ever so good."

"Please don't take him away," Emilia pleaded. "We have been taking good care of him, I promise!"

"Please, Miss Bennet, say we can keep him!" Sophia joined in.

"Uncle Thomas doesn't need to know," added Emilia. "It can be our secret."

Mary blinked at their words and shook herself free from her stupor. "No," she said firmly. "This cannot be kept a secret. I have to tell Mr. Bowen. You may plead your case with him, and he may decide whether or not you can keep the puppy."

The girls fell silent, shocked by her sharp words. They stayed planted by the toy chest as she strode decidedly for the bell-pull and waited impatiently for someone to respond to her summons, tapping one foot anxiously.

When one of the maids finally peeked in after what seemed like an eternity to the nervous girls, Mary said briskly, "Please tell Mr. Bowen that I request his presence in the nursery. Tell him it is urgent."

The maid curtseyed and hurried off to do her bidding. Mary came back to join the girls at the chest. The puppy, having tired of yipping, was now standing on his back legs, scratching at the sides of the chest and trying to climb out.

Emilia reached in to pick him up, but Mary stayed her with a hand on her arm. "No. Leave him where he is, please."

It seemed like an interminably long time until Thomas finally appeared at the door. Mary looked up at his knock and stepped away from the chest to greet him. "Mr. Bowen, thank you for coming up. I apologize for interrupting your morning."

"It was no imposition, Miss Bennet," Thomas hastened to assure her. "How can I be of service?"

Mary hesitated. "I think you had better see for yourself." She pointed him to the toy chest and he crossed the room curiously to peer inside.

The girls waited anxiously for his reaction, hoping for the best.

Thomas blinked. Then he looked at the girls, still standing by the toy chest as they waited for him to speak. "Are those my cravats?" he asked painfully, hoping he was wrong, but fearing he already knew the answer.

Sophia looked even guiltier. "Perhaps."

"How did-" He held up one hand as she would have started to explain. "Never mind. It does not matter." He took a deep breath and let it out with a whoosh. "Well, one thing is for certain. He must go back to his mother."

The girls broke down at his words.

"No, Uncle Thomas!" Emilia sobbed. "Please don't take him away!"

"Don't take Duke away!" Sophia shrieked, throwing herself at Thomas and clinging to his trouser leg. "I love him!"

John walked in on them as they were in the midst of the chaos. "I say, what is all this noise about?" He espied his uncle and the girls by the toy chest and immediately discerned what was going on. He threw himself between the chest and Thomas. "You can't take Duke away from us! It's not fair!"

Thomas tried to be heard above the din in an attempt to talk some sense into the children, but it was an impossible task. He looked over at Mary and shrugged, sharing an exasperated glance. He turned back to the children. "Now see here-"

He was not allowed to finish. John snatched the puppy from the toy chest. "If you won't let us keep Duke, then I'm not staying here! I hate you!" He turned on his heel and bolted from the room.

"Me neither!" declared Sophia and ran out behind him as fast as her short legs would carry her, Emilia right behind her.

Thomas and Mary were left standing in shock as the door banged shut behind the children. Mary eyed Thomas with trepidation as he ran one hand irritably through his hair, frustrated. "Well, that did not go quite like I had hoped," he said.

"Do you think we should go after them?" she asked.

"Undoubtedly," he responded. "But let us give them a few minutes to cool off first, or we will never get that puppy away from them." He sank down into one of the child-sized chairs the girls had abandoned and sighed, rubbing his hands over his eyes. "I was just going to tell them the puppy needed to be returned to its mother until it was old enough to be on its own. I was going to let them keep it."

Mary took the seat across from him. "You would have let them keep him, even though they lied and hid him from you?"

Thomas chuckled wryly. "Yes, and I still will. Every child needs a dog to grow up with. Ironically, I had already decided to let them choose a puppy out of that litter when the pups were weaned. They just got a little ahead of me."

Mary shook her head in wonder. "You are a very kind man, Mr. Bowen."

"Thomas," he corrected her abruptly. "My name is Thomas."

She ducked her head shyly and peeped up at him from under her lashes. "Very well then… Thomas."

He grinned at her, pleased with her acquiescence. "Am I to be granted the same liberty, Miss Bennet?"

She smiled back and answered timidly, "If you wish."

"Ah, but it is not what I wish, but what you wish that matters."

"Well, then, what I wish is that we go after those children before they have the opportunity to get very far."

"You are probably right," Thomas agreed. "Given the time, they could almost disappear on the property." He pushed back his chair and stood, offering Mary a hand up. "I have to locate my overcoat and boots before we go traipsing about the estate after the children. Shall we meet in the entry in say, five minutes or so?"

"I think that can be arranged."

"Very well. I shall see you then." He left her with a bow to see to it. Mary gathered up her own outerwear and headed down the stairs to wait for him. At least she could do no further damage to her petticoat. It was already beyond repair.

A few short minutes later, he came bounding down the stairs to join her. "I informed Bertram that the children had run off again. He is organizing some of the servants into a search party, but I thought perhaps we could check some of their regular hiding places together."

"That sounds like a suitable plan," Mary agreed.

They set off on the same route they had traveled the week before when the children had run off.

"At least you do not have to worry about Helene joining her brother and sisters yet and running off," Mary commented as they walked.

Thomas laughed. "Yes. I am grateful that she is still young enough that she cannot defy me as well. At least it is one less to worry about at the moment. I rue the day when she can join her siblings." He shook his head. "Of course, she will probably be the worst one of the bunch."

Mary silently agreed. They all spoiled the little darling terribly, but she was so sweet and adorable they just could not seem to help it.

Mary's steps slowed as they neared their first stop, the cave Thomas had disappeared into the week before. She eyed the man beside her. Would he expect her to accompany him inside?

Thomas did not hesitate as he crossed to the opening. Apparently, he had not remembered her dislike of small, dark places. Mary took a deep breath and followed him inside, attempting to dredge up some courage as the darkness swallowed her.

She bumped into Thomas' back as her eyes struggled to adjust to the dim lighting. He steadied her with one hand as he looked around, checking for any signs that the children had been there.

Mary shivered in the dank, clammy air. A thin band of light illuminated the entrance, but not much else. The cave was small, as Thomas had said it was. She could barely stand up straight within its confines, and Thomas had to stoop to fit.

A bead of moisture from the ceiling dripped on to the back of her neck and coursed its way under her collar. She shuddered under its cool touch and shifted a step closer to Thomas. The walls of the cave seemed to be pressing in on her. She swallowed hard against the terror that was beginning to well in her chest and took a deep breath to settle her nerves. She sidled nearer to Thomas. Unexpectedly, she felt something drop on to her shoulder and begin crawling up her neck.

Mary shrieked and swiped at her neck, jumping back into Thomas and sending them both sprawling on to the floor of the cave. She flailed, still feeling a thousand creeping legs crawling all over her, and managed to land a few solid blows to Thomas' abdomen and shoulders in the process. A wayward knee very nearly caught him in a delicate area.

He ducked to avoid an elbow to his temple and wrapped his arms around her to stop her thrashing about so. "Mary! Mary! Calm down! It is all right! What in the world happened?"

She trembled in his arms and his heart wrenched.

"I th-think a spider fell on me," she managed to stutter out.

He tried to respond calmly, knowing she would feed off his emotions. "Where did it fall?"

"On m-my n-neck." She was crying now, from the shock of it all.

"All right then, let me just check to make sure you got it off," he said soothingly. He felt her nod against his chest and slowly raised one hand to push aside the hair that had come tumbling down in their fall to inspect her neck.

He ran his hand over the smooth, graceful curve of her neck and, when he found nothing, cupped her cheek tenderly in his hand. "I think it is gone," he reassured her. "There is nothing to be frightened of now."

She sniffed and he felt her press her cheek into his palm as she nodded.

He dropped his hand and gave her one last comforting squeeze before he pulled back. He helped her to her feet and glanced around them. "I do not see any signs of the children. Shall we move on before any other creatures decide to bother us?" He smiled as he spoke, trying to lighten the mood.

She sniffed again and rubbed her sleeve across her eyes to wipe away her tears. "I should like that very much."

She followed him outside and he could sense the relief washing over her as they stepped back into the light. She smiled weakly. "Thank you, Mr. Bowen. I apologize for such an unseemly display. I do hope I have not hurt you?"

"I am perfectly well," he reassured her. "And it is Thomas, remember?"

Her smile turned shy. "Yes, Thomas."

He offered her his arm. "We had better get a move on. There are many more hiding places we have yet to search."

*****

John, Emilia, and Sophia huddled together against the base of a classically garbed statue in the grotto. They had traveled farther into the depths of the estate than they had ever ventured.

Duke had exhausted himself running in circles around the statue and had collapsed at their feet, worn out.

Sophia laid her head on Emilia's shoulder. "Do you think they are looking for us?"

John snorted. "Of course they are looking for us, silly. What else would they be doing?" He folded his arms stubbornly. "I hope they never find us."

"What are we going to do?" Emilia said. "We don't have anywhere else to go." She gestured at the stone walls around them. "We can't live here."

"We'll go back to Portsmouth."

"How are you going to do that?" Emilia asked sarcastically. "That is miles away. And even if we do manage to make it there, Pappa is at sea, and there is no one else to care for us but Uncle Thomas. Maybe we should go back to the house." She peered at the lengthening shadows as the daylight faded. "It is getting awful late."

John did not want to admit that she was right. It was a lost cause and he knew it, but he was not quite ready to admit defeat and head back. He was too stubborn to let his Uncle Thomas win that easily. He was going to have to find them if he wanted them to come back.

He stroked the puppy's silky fur where it laid against his leg and shivered in the cool, damp air of the grotto.

Sophia snuggled closer to Emilia. "I'm cold and I'm hungry and I don't want to walk all the way back to Portsmouth. I hope they find us soon." She sniffled and swiped her hand over her dripping nose.

John heard the tears threatening in her voice. His little sister was on the verge of a meltdown. He had pushed them to make it this far in so short a period of time and Sophia was showing the effects of that exertion. Even Emilia looked weary. She draped one arm around her sister's shoulders and gave her a comforting squeeze, shooting her brother a disgruntled glare over Sophia's head.

John shifted uncomfortably under her gaze and looked away. It was not his fault the girls had followed him. They could have just as easily stayed at the house with Uncle Thomas. Still, as the girls cuddled together to stay warm, his mother's last words to him echoed in his mind.

Take care of your sisters, John. They look to you to lead them. They need you to look out for them.

Her voice had been too weak to lift above a whisper and she had trailed off into a fit of coughing after just those few sentences. She had tried to hide it, but John had noticed that the handkerchief she had put to her lips was stained with blood.

She had patted his arm comfortingly when she saw the fear in his eyes, too weary from coughing to speak, but it had done no good. He knew she was dying.

Two days later, she was gone.

John burrowed his chin a little deeper into his collar to ward off the chill. Emilia was right. There was nothing left for them in Portsmouth. Even when their father did return from sea, he would only be on shore for a short time before he sailed off again. It was the way of a sailor's life. Their father would just send them back to Kaverstow to live.

He was smart enough to know he could not care for the girls on his own. Young ladies required governesses and dresses and seasons in Town. His mother had dreamed of all those things for his sisters and had giddily prepared for the day they emerged into polite society. No, they were better off with their Uncle Thomas. Even if the man was a little clueless at times, he had taken steps to provide for them. He had even gotten the girls a governess and was teaching him how to run Kaverstow. It was probably more than his parents had ever hoped for them.

He debated returning to the house, worried that the girls might become ill from exposure to the night air. He stood to pace to the grotto opening, peering out as dusk began to descend upon them. There was only one problem with that plan. In his haste to put distance between them and the house, he had run blindly, not paying attention to the direction he was traveling.

He had no idea how to get back.

*****

Thomas was really beginning to worry as dusk settled around them.

He and Mary had checked all of the children's normal hiding places, to no avail. They had traveled farther than either of them had intended to, their desperation mounting as each place they checked turned up empty.

Thomas glanced at Mary from the corner of his eye. He could tell she was flagging. She gamely kept pace with him, but weariness seeped from her core, manifesting itself in the sagging of her shoulders and the drooping of her eyelids. If they did not find the children soon he was going to have to insist she return to the house for her own well-being.

He continued to study her as they walked. Her head was down, on the lookout for any tripping hazards, making it easy to observe her unnoticed. She had tried to restore order to her hair after the incident in the cave, but had given up the effort as futile.

The fine, wispy strands framed her delicate features, drawing his attention to her luminous eyes. He had never noticed how expressive they were before now. Their depths reflected her exhaustion, but mostly they shone with worry for the children.

He reached over silently to grasp her cold fingers with his own, squeezing her hand reassuringly. She glanced up at his touch to smile wearily back at him before she returned her gaze to the ground. But she did not let go of his hand, and his heart warmed a little at the realization.

They continued searching, walking hand-in-hand.

After an indeterminate amount of time, Mary drew to a halt, tugging Thomas to a stop beside her. He looked over at her questioningly.

"Where are we headed?" Mary asked. "Do you have a certain place in mind or are we wandering aimlessly?"

"We have looked in all the usual places," he admitted. "But there is one more I think we should look. There is a grotto on the property that would make a perfect hiding spot.

As far as I know, the children have never been there, but it is somewhere I think we should try looking."

Mary nodded and they resumed walking.

Darkness was almost upon them when they finally reached the grotto. After the incident in the cave earlier, Thomas thought it better to leave Mary outside as he investigated. He reluctantly let go of her hand, instantly missing its presence in his own.

Mary watched him as he disappeared inside, wondering at the sudden sense of loss she was left with when he had removed his hand from off hers. She stretched her fingers, still feeling the pressure of his hand around hers.

She looked around her, seeking a distraction from the warmth that flooded her at the thought of holding hands with Thomas Bowen. The man had no idea the havoc he was wreaking on her equilibrium.

The light was fading quickly. Already, she could barely make out the grotto entrance. She worried about Thomas bumbling about in the cave in the dark and hurting himself, about the children lost about the estate, and about making the trek back in the dark. She hoped Thomas knew his estate well enough to guide them back to the house safely. She nibbled on the corner of her thumbnail as she waited, impatient for his return. If he did not come out soon, she was going to have to go in after him and she *really* did not want to have to do that, especially in the dark.

Just when she had decided she should go in after him, he emerged from the grotto, victorious. He was carrying an exhausted Sophia wrapped in his overcoat, with Emilia and John following behind him with the puppy.

Mary rushed forward to embrace them, awash with relief at finding them safe. "Thank goodness we found you! Are you all alright?" She looked them up and down for any signs of injury, brushing her hands over their arms to reassure herself they were fine.

Emilia nodded with a weak smile. "Just cold and hungry."

Thomas smiled at Mary's motherly reaction and pointed to their clothing. "And dirty."

Mary sent him a quick smile before she turned her attention back to the children. "I should think we can remedy those ailments fairly easily."

"Just as soon as we get back to the house," Thomas reminded them all. "We had better start back."

"You are right, of course," Mary agreed briskly, taking Emilia's hand and pulling John up to walk between Thomas and her. There was no way she was letting the boy out of her sight.

The trek back to the house was long and arduous, and they were all exhausted by the time they made it back. The butler and the housekeeper were waiting by the door for them as they came in. Mary and Thomas handed the shivering children over to the nurse and housekeeper to be taken upstairs for baths and Thomas confiscated the puppy that John would have absconded with upstairs. "I will take that, young man. Go upstairs, take your bath, and eat your dinner. We will discuss the matter further tomorrow."

John reluctantly trudged up the steps, sending one last despairing glance over his shoulder at Duke.

Thomas turned to Mary as the children disappeared from view, his face reflecting the same fatigue she felt. Still, he managed to dredge up a wry smile. "If nothing else, I think today has shown me you were right about setting some rules. I will have to get on that." He sighed and ran a hand through his rumpled hair. "It is far too late for you to be traveling home. Let me send a servant to collect your things and deliver a message to your father. You can stay in one of the guest bedrooms tonight."

Mary agreed without hesitation. She was past the point of caring about her reputation. All she wanted was a hot bath of her own, a bite to eat, and a warm bed to enfold her.

With her acceptance of the invitation, Thomas looked at the butler. "You will see to it, will you not, Bertram? Please make sure Miss Bennet has everything she needs."

The butler bowed. "Certainly, sir."

Thomas turned his attention back to Mary, smiling down at her wearily. "Breakfast is served at 8:00 a.m., Miss Bennet. I look forward to seeing you then." He bowed over the hand she offered him with her thanks and disappeared upstairs, leaving her watching the butler expectantly.

Bertram bowed and gestured for her to follow him. "Just this way, Miss Bennet."

*****

Mary sank gratefully into the plush folds of the bed, sighing in pleasure at the luxury that engulfed her. Warm from her bath and with her hunger satiated, she slid easily into slumber.

Thomas did not find sleep so easily. Thoughts of Mary Bennet in his house, asleep just a floor away, plagued him. He could easily imagine her dark tresses spread over the white pillow. The mental image was a captivating one.

What would it be like, to have her here always, sharing his heart and his home?

His thoughts startled him. When had Mary Bennet gone from his employee to someone he could envision spending his life with? He could not pinpoint the day or the hour. But now, just the thought of her as his wife coaxed a smile to his lips. Somehow, she had slipped into his life and made a place for herself without his even realizing it was happening.

The question was, now that he knew he had feelings for her, what was he going to do about it?

CHAPTER NINE

The first order of business, Thomas decided upon waking, was to determine if there were any signs Miss Bennet might share his feelings.

This was not as easy a task as he had assumed it would be.

He readied himself to go down to breakfast with unusual care. His valet was delighted, but Thomas fretted over every step of the process.

Was his attire too formal, or not formal enough? Should his cravat be tied in the Waterfall style or the Oriental? A black waistcoat or blue? There were too many decisions to be made and he agonized over each of them.

Finally, he was ready, with just enough time to spare to make it down to the breakfast room at precisely eight o'clock. He was pleased upon entering to find that Mary was already there.

She was seated at the table with a plate full of toast and fruit, the paper in one hand and her coffee cup in the other. She raised her cup to take a sip as he watched, her eyes never leaving the page she held.

Thomas smiled at the sight and went over to the buffet to fill his own plate and pour himself a cup of steaming coffee. He settled into the seat across from Mary and cleared his throat to get her attention.

She looked up with a start and he grinned. "I hope you slept well, Miss Bennet."

She smiled back. "I did, thank you."

"Was everything to your liking?"

"It was."

This was more difficult than he had realized it would be. He was struggling to keep her attention. Already her gaze had wandered back to look longingly at the paper she had laid beside her plate upon his arrival. He searched his mind for something, *anything*, to keep her speaking with him.

"Have you found something to interest you in the papers?"

Mary smiled widely, caressing the paper with one hand. "Nothing in particular. I am just enjoying the novelty of actually being able to read the paper over breakfast. At Longbourn, my father always makes off with it for his own use. Lizzy was the only one who could pry it away from him."

Thomas grinned, finally understanding her distraction and relieved that it had nothing to do with him. "By all means then, do not let me detain you. Read!"

Her smile was tinged with gratitude as she gave the paper a shake and spread it open before her, eagerly scanning the print.

Thomas was content to watch her unobserved as she read. He had plenty of time to determine her feelings toward him, he realized. With a little cunning, he could arrange time with her nearly every day she was at his home, and for those days when she was not, he could count on her mother to work in his favor. If he was determined to pursue Mary

Bennet it would be easily done, even if Miss Bennet did not know it yet.

Thomas watched as Mary's brow furrowed in concentration, one hand spearing a piece of fruit absentmindedly with her fork and lifting it to her lips. He was tempted to let his gaze linger on her mouth, but he recognized the dangerous direction those thoughts would lead him in and instead dragged his eyes away to study the rest of her.

She wore a lavender morning dress he was sure he had never seen her in before. He smiled as he recognized her mother's machinations in the choice. The soft color drew the green from her eyes and put color in her cheeks in a way the grays and whites Mary seemed to prefer never did. The dress was still only really notable for its simplicity, but the neckline seemed a little lower than what was usual for her and she had a lace fichu tucked into the bodice to camouflage the fact.

Her hair was different this morning as well, he realized. His household did not generally require the use of a ladies' maid, but one of the maids had obviously been pressed into service by Bertram and the results were charming.

Instead of being pulled back into a severe bun, her tresses were curled and piled on top of her head in the most appealing disarray. He could not quite decide if the effect was intentional or the result of some poor maid's disastrous attempts.

Regardless, she looked rather fetching, especially for someone he should ostensibly still be thinking of as his children's governess.

Mary folded the paper and glanced up to catch him staring at her. She worriedly put a hand up to her hair under his scrutiny, checking that it had not come undone. "Is there something wrong?"

"No, no," Thomas hastened to reassure her. "Everything is just fine. I was just admiring your hairstyle. You have done something different with it, have you not?"

Mary blushed. "Yes. I would have done it myself in my usual fashion, but the maid that attended me this morning was insistent that she should do the honors. After she had expended so much effort getting it just so, I could not bring myself to rearrange it."

Thomas studied the curls. "Perhaps you should wear your hair like that more often. It suits you."

The flush that covered her cheeks deepened. "I am pleased you approve. I would not want my employer to think me too brazen."

Thomas was startled by her proclamation and without thinking blurted, "Never! I do not think the word brazen could ever be used in conjunction with you, Miss Bennet." He shifted awkwardly in his seat as a flush started up the back of his neck. "Brazen comes from the Old English word *bræsen* which is derived from the word *bræs*, or "brass," and suggests a face unable to show shame; one that has been hardened. You, my dear Miss Bennet, could only be considered the most gentle of women, as your conduct towards my nieces and nephew attests."

Mary stared at him, her expression unreadable, as he finished his speech. Thomas silently cursed himself. Once again he had bored where he had meant to compliment. Would he never learn that his knowledge of etymology was unwelcome? He picked up his coffee cup and drank in an attempt to hide his discomfort.

When he set his cup back down, she was still staring at him.

"Thank you, Mr. Bowen," she said slowly. "That is perhaps the kindest thing anyone has ever said to me."

"Thomas," he blurted. "Remember, I told you to call me Thomas."

Her smile bloomed and her eyes softened. "I remember... Thomas. And if I am to be on such informal terms with you, then you must be so as well. Please, call me Mary, at least so long as we are not in polite company."

His smile mirrored hers. "I should like that very much."

They sat, grinning at each other for an indeterminate amount of time before Thomas suddenly recollected himself. Pulling out his watch, he checked the hour and was shocked to see that so much time had passed since he had come down to breakfast.

He pushed back his chair with a start and stood to grace Mary with a bow. "You must excuse me, Miss Bennet. The hour has grown later than I had realized and I have a meeting with my steward to attend to. Perhaps I shall see you after luncheon in the gardens?"

Mary smiled up at him, her cheeks colored with the lightest shade of pink, her pleasure at his suggestion reflected in her eyes. "I think it very likely."

Warmth and delight surged through Thomas at her response. "I shall look forward to it with the greatest of anticipation." With a last bow, he left her to finish her meal and join the children.

*****

Mary hurried the girls through their luncheon. She was looking forward to their excursion into the gardens with unbridled enthusiasm. Her cheeks flushed just remembering the way Mr. Bowen...Thomas... had looked at her that morning, and the compliment he had paid her.

If she did not know better she would almost say there had been something akin to interest in his eyes. But that was impossible. She was plain Mary Bennet, the daughter her mother despaired of ever seeing married. Even Mr. Collins had not thought her worthy of his notice as a prospective spouse, and that ridiculous toad had certainly set his sights on almost every other available woman in the area.

No, it was far more likely that it was exhaustion that had him looking at her like that. Perhaps he had been seeing double in his tired state.

The girls were quickly bundled into their warm clothes and ushered outside. Mary directed them into the gardens, careful to keep them in the open areas where she could keep a close eye on them. It was not long before Thomas and John joined them. John ran ahead to play with his sisters while Thomas came to stand quietly beside Mary.

"How was your morning?" asked Mary when he failed to greet her.

"Hmmm?" he said, distracted. "Oh." He shrugged as her words registered. "It was uneventful other than John's constant inquiries about Duke. I told him I was going to wait until we could all discuss the matter together before I spoke to him about it. He was not too happy about that, but there it is."

"I can well imagine. What are you going to tell them?"

"The same thing I told you yesterday. Duke needs to be with his mother for at least a few more weeks. After that we can discuss having him in the house and who will care for him and such things."

"I think that will be a far less painful response for them than what they are expecting you to say."

Thomas grinned crookedly. "I should suppose so. If they had just let me finish yesterday we might have been able to avoid all the worry and heartache."

"Patience is not a strong virtue for most children."

"No," he said absently, his gaze on the children. "It is not."

She sensed his distraction with the upcoming discussion and fell silent, her own gaze fixed on the girls as they chased each other across the lawn.

They let the children play until they tired and returned to them of their own volition. Then they settled everyone down on nearby benches to finish the discussion Duke's discovery had started the day before.

Mary put her arm around Sophia, who had snuggled in beside her, while Emilia and John perched on the bench next to them. Thomas rose to pace before the benches, his mind obviously preoccupied with how to start the conversation.

Finally, he halted in front of them and began to speak, his words tumbling forth in a rush that attested to his discomfort with the situation. "I am aware of how very fond you all have grown of Duke in such a short period of time. I have no desire to deprive you of him entirely, as I feel strongly that every child should have a pet at some point in their life. However, I cannot ignore the way you have gone about acquiring your pet."

He fixed his gaze on each of the children in turn. "You have disregarded my authority as your guardian, you have put yourselves in harm's way- and thereby also Miss Bennet and me and the rest of the household- and you have deliberately disobeyed me."

The children squirmed under his intense gaze.

"I cannot condone such behavior, and I think your mother would be appalled to know the way you have conducted yourselves." He paused for effect, letting his words sink into his young listeners. All three of their faces paled at the mention of their mother in connection with their behavior, and Emilia sniffled loudly.

"That having been said," He went on, his tone gentling, "I have no qualms about allowing you to have Duke as a pet." He held up a hand to stay them when their countenances brightened and they would have jumped up to embrace him. "But I do have some rules. And they are nonnegotiable. If I at any time discern that they are not being followed, Duke will be sent back to the kennel with the other hounds, no questions asked and no squabbling over it."

The children were all nodding eagerly, heads bobbing in unison. Mary bit back a smile at their eager anticipation and willingness to agree with everything he said.

"First of all, Duke is not quite old enough to be separated from his mother and brothers and sisters for very long. He needs to stay with them in the stables for at least a few more weeks. Secondly, if you discern that Duke needs to go outside, at any time, for obvious reasons, then you are to find Bertram, who will assist you with that. Also, he is to be trained so that he does not disturb any company that we may have. I will not have a pet disrupt our guests' comfort. If it becomes evident that Duke cannot behave himself around company, then he will be sent to the kennels for the duration of the visit. I also withhold the right to make any necessary changes to said rules should the need arise. Am I understood?"

"Yes, Uncle Thomas!" The girls bounded up from their seats to hug him, squealing with pleasure, while John hung back, too old for such unseemly displays of affection.

Thomas looked up over their heads to meet Mary's eyes. She smiled warmly at him, her eyes shining with approval.

Warmth flooded through him at her obvious approval of how he had handled the situation. Mayhap, he was finally beginning to get this parenting thing right!

When the girls finally started to quiet down, Thomas put them away from him and smiled down at their happy faces. "Now, who would be interested in a visit to Duke in the stables?"

His suggestion was met with yet more noise and shrieking, but Thomas did not mind. He just grinned. It was worth the decibel level to know that his nieces and nephew were happy.

He sent the children on ahead, preferring instead to linger behind with Miss Bennet as they walked the path down to the stables.

"Did you have a dog of your own once?" Mary asked curiously as they walked. When he glanced up at her in surprise at the personal question, she hastened to add, "I only ask because you seem so determined that the children should have a pet."

Thomas smiled. "I did, once. He was my best friend growing up. It was just Anne and I, you see, and my mother insisted that Anne should not be traipsing about with me, ruining her clothes. So we did everything together, Abner and I."

Mary stifled a smile with a hand over her mouth. "Abner?"

"Yes," Thomas said. "Do you find the name humorous?"

"Not at all," Mary said. "I just find it a rather odd choice for a little boy. It is so... *mature*."

"It is, is it not? I did not choose it. By the time Abner came to be mine he had already led a rather fulfilled life as one of my father's hunting dogs. He was injured during a hunt and my father decided that rather than put him down he should become my companion."

"That was well-done of him."

"I certainly thought so. It was probably the single greatest gift any person has ever given me. I have never been one that was particularly comfortable amongst society, but Abner loved me just the way I was. I did not have to worry about saying the wrong thing while in his company or offending him. I was very fond of him."

"What became of him?"

"What you would expect. He lived to a ripe old age and passed away peacefully when I was about fifteen."

"And you have not had a dog since?"

"No, not in the same way. The estate has hounds and such, but I do not keep a dog as a pet."

"Why not? I would think that the experience would have persuaded you to try again."

Thomas smiled crookedly. "Perhaps I might yet. But at the moment, I have more than enough trouble on my hands with my sister's children and their new puppy."

Mary laughed. "That is true." She turned her gaze back to the gravel path they traveled. "I wish I had known such a childhood. My sisters and I had a cat, but the silly beast preferred Lydia over us all."

"What an odd preference."

His comment brought Mary's head up. She grinned widely at him, her eyes shining with pleasure at his response and his obvious dislike for Lydia. Warmth spread in his gut at her reaction. He was ridiculously pleased with himself for having made her smile so.

"It is especially strange given Lydia's penchant as a child for stepping on its tail and pulling its fur. But Lydia has always had a way of making people and animals like her despite her faults. I have never understood it."

Thomas nodded sagely. "I have noticed that. Your mother is particularly fond of her, I believe."

Mary nodded mutely, the subject beginning to touch a little too close to home for further comment.

Thomas instinctively knew this, and changed the subject, much to her relief. "Perhaps someday, when you have a home of your own, you may have a dog of your own as well."

Mary smiled up at him, her eyes holding a hint of uncertainty and sadness that confused him. "Perhaps." He could not know that although she hoped for such a future, it was far from guaranteed.

She studied the man before her and wished for what she could not have. Thomas Bowen would never look at her as more than an employee. It was too much for a girl like her to hope for.

The gravel path gave way to the stables and Thomas sighed. Their time alone together was almost up and he was no closer to knowing her feelings than he had been when he got up that morning. She was inclined to enjoy his company, he believed, but was that enough? He needed to know more, to observe her closely and decipher each glance and word. He needed to know how she was with other men; if there was a competitor for her hand.

From her mother's actions he would suppose not, but perhaps she held a secret tendre for some other man. He had to know, and the only way to do so would be to appear in society where she would be also. He steeled himself to go through with the idea, as repugnant as it was to him.

There was an assembly coming up in a fortnight's time, and although he had had no prior intentions of attending, he did now.

As they crossed the stable yard, he turned to his companion, drawing her to a halt beside him. "Will you be attending the coming assembly?"

She looked up at him in surprise at the sudden question. "I will be."

"May I request the honor of your hand for the first two dances?"

Her cheeks flushed crimson and her heart skipped a beat at the earnest entreaty in his eyes. "I should like that very much."

With that, they were at the door. They stepped inside and were greeted by three enthusiastic children and a pen full of raucous puppies. There was no further opportunity for private conversation, but Thomas was not terribly disappointed.

He shared a glance with Mary over the pen and grinned widely when she looked away, her cheeks pink. If her blush was any indication, he had much to be optimistic about.

CHAPTER TEN

A fortnight flew by. Thomas was careful to ingratiate himself into Mary's days at Kaverstow. They had a very fruitful discussion that resulted in some pertinent rules being set and their days becoming a little easier. They often met in the hall as she came in the mornings and as she left at night, and their afternoons were spent together in the gardens, ostensibly for the children's sake, but in reality for their own enjoyment as well.

Thomas was pleased with the progress he had made. He felt reasonably certain that Mary held him in some esteem. Their time together, while not dominated by witty repartee, was full of pleasant conversation and laughter that gave him insight into the depth of her character. It was easy for him to picture a life with them together.

They would be a ready-made family with his sister's four children, but he could see the love Mary had for them already. It would only continue to grow as they spent more time in close company. She would make them a wonderful mother figure, and perhaps eventually they would be able to add their own children to the brood. Lord knows they would have to add on to the house if they did, but it would be worth it.

Every day in her company painted the picture just a little more clearly for him. The future stood before him, bright and clear, just waiting for the taking. And he was not about to let the opportunity pass him by.

*****

The assembly rooms were crowded and hot, the scents of alcohol and perfume overpowering in the stale air. Mary Bennet fanned herself vigorously, trying to dispel the nausea that rose in her stomach.

It was almost time for the dancing to begin, and her gaze hungrily sought Thomas among the crowd. She had seen him come in just a few moments ago. He had reminded her of his promised two dances that morning and she was all together too pleased to grant them to him.

It was becoming difficult to hide her growing attraction to her handsome employer. Two weeks in close company had taught her to hope in a way she had never thought to. Sometimes she would glance up and catch him watching her with the most indecipherable look in his eyes. Her heart raced just thinking about it and she was glad for the white gloves that hid her sweaty palms.

She caught sight of Thomas across the dance floor and gave him a demure wave. He smiled at her and started over, his eyes never leaving her face.

Mary felt herself growing pink under his intense gaze. She smoothed one hand over her up-do and hoped he approved of the way she looked. She had taken particular care with her toilette that day and agonized over choosing a gown. Her gown was demure but fashionable and she had instructed Hill to the best of her ability in how to recreate the hairstyle Thomas had complimented her on when she had spent the night at Kaverstow.

He was before her now, bowing over her hand. "Miss Bennet, you look absolutely lovely this evening."

She was *definitely* blushing now, but that did not stop a silly grin from spreading over her face at the glint of approval in his eyes. "Thank you, Mr. Bowen."

"I am looking forward to our dances."

"As am I."

They threatened to descend into silence, lost in each other's eyes. Fortunately, the band chose that moment to begin to play, and Thomas offered her his hand. "Shall we?"

They were halfway through the first set when a commotion at the far end of the room brought the dancing to a halt.

"What is it?" whispered Mary to Thomas, unable to see over the crowd of people what had caused the disruption.

"I say, it rather looks like a couple of gentlemen and a lady," he whispered back.

"Really?" Mary strained to see over the heads of her neighbors, but it was pointless. Her petite stature kept her from even getting a glance. The newcomers moved off to the side and the band started up again. The dancers took their places and resumed where they had left off. "Well, I daresay Mamma will have found out all the gossip about them by the time the set is over anyway."

Thomas laughed. "Yes. We can count on her to be well-informed."

They finished the set and Mary allowed Thomas to lead her to her seat beside her mother. He went off in search of refreshments for them both.

Mrs. Bennet was all aflutter.

"Come, Mamma, what is the matter?" Mary asked, aware her mother was anxious to spread the knowledge she had already gleaned from her acquaintances.

"Oh, Mary! You are saved at last!"

Mary was rather startled by this proclamation. "I was not aware, Mamma, that I needed saving."

Mrs. Bennet sniffed. "Well, you should not have, if that insufferable Mr. Bowen had made you an offer already."

Mary glanced around her, praying Thomas had not been near enough to hear that comment and relieved to find he was across the room at the punch bowl. "Mamma!" she protested. "He is my employer!"

Mrs. Bennet waved away her objections. "Yes, yes. But you had much better have a husband! And what a fine husband you shall have!" She smiled and clapped her hands together happily.

Dread gathered in the pit of Mary's stomach. "Whatever are you speaking of?"

Mrs. Bennet pointed out a man Mary had hitherto not noticed. "Netherfield Park has been let at last! By Mr. Simmons. A single man of large fortune; eight or nine thousand a year. What a fine thing for you, Mary! You must know that I am thinking of his marrying you."

Mary remembered a remarkably similar conversation not too long ago that involved another young man of fine fortune and was not comforted. "Mamma! I have not even been introduced to the man! You cannot speak of such things."

"That most certainly can be easily remedied. See! Here comes your father now! We shall have him introduce us, for I saw him not ten minutes ago making Mr. Simmons' acquaintance." She put her hand up to catch her husband's attention. "Mr. Bennet! Mr. Bennet!"

Mary was mortified by her mother's unseemly display and sought a way to stop it. "Should we not wait for Lydia to be introduced as well?"

Mrs. Bennet waved away her objections. "Nonsense! Lydia is dancing. Besides, *she* has already found herself a husband!" She waved her arm more vigorously as Mr. Bennet attempted to ignore his wife. "MR. BENNET!"

Mary soon thereafter found herself being reluctantly dragged along behind her parents in order to be introduced to the gentleman and his party.

Thomas watched her go, having finally secured refreshments for them. He took a sip from his glass and watched as she made her curtsey.

He, too, had heard the gossip about Mr. Simmons. The man was a most eligible catch, and he should be pleased for Mary at the frank appreciation he saw in the man's face as he was introduced to her. But he could not be happy by the appearance of a possible rival for her hand.

He was all too aware that the man had much to offer her. His own five thousand a year could not compare to nine thousand and Netherfield Park. He could not offer her the carriages and pin money and undivided attention that Mr. Simmons could as a single man. All he could give her were four rambunctious children and an obnoxious puppy with a habit of chewing on the furniture. What comparison could there be? Surely, she must see that.

A night that had begun with such joy and hope was now overshadowed by doubts. *Still*, he squared his shoulders as Mary and her parents left Mr. Simmons to find their seats again, *all was not lost*. He would not give up so easily. Mr. Simmons was going to have to fight him for Mary's affections if he wanted her.

He took another gulp from his glass for some liquid courage and crossed the dance floor to join her.

He handed Mary the other glass he held and watched as she sipped the beverage gratefully. "I see your mother wasted no time in making the introductions." Thomas was gratified by the furrow that appeared between her brows.

"She is never one to allow an opportunity slip by."

"How did you find Mr. Simmons? I have not yet had the pleasure of making his acquaintance."

Mary shrugged. "He seems most amiable, I suppose. There was not much opportunity for discussion, as he was very much in demand."

"I imagine he would be."

Thomas would have happily spent the rest of the assembly in Mary's company, but lingering any longer would have left even the most discreet of the gossips with their tongues wagging. He waited until she had finished her glass before he took his leave. "I see a gentleman I simply must speak with in the corner over there, but I hope you will save me the supper set?"

Mary happily agreed, although she was sure her mother would have preferred she reserve them for Mr. Simmons, just in case by some strange coincidence he should solicit her hand for them. But as she had much rather spend the set dancing with Thomas, she was more than willing to promise him what he asked.

Having secured her hand, Thomas absconded to a distant corner of the room that gave him a fine prospect of Mary and entered into a lively discussion about farming methods with the gentleman beside him.

It was not long before movement in Mary's direction caught his eye. Mr. Simmons was bowing over Mary's hand and leading her on to the dance floor.

Thomas' companion was prattling on, but he was no longer attending to his words. His entire attention was focused on Mary and Mr. Simmons, winding in and out among the other couples on the dance floor.

He had to admit they made a handsome couple, with Mr. Simmons dark head bent solicitously over Mary's curls, but the sting of jealousy was already rearing its ugly head. He squelched the urge to rush across the dance floor and whisk

Mary away from Mr. Simmons and off into his arms. The desire was hardly proper. Moreover, he reminded himself, Mary had the right to decide her own future, regardless of how he might try to influence her.

She was bright, and beautiful, and she was sure to attract the attention of other gentlemen wherever she might go. She could do far better than him, as was already evidenced by Mr. Simmons' interest. He was fortunate that she had never traveled far enough from Hertfordshire to attract too much male attention, or she surely would never have looked twice at him.

His companion had paused in his speech and was eyeing him strangely. Thomas hurried to cover over any awkwardness, surmising that he must have been asked a question to which he had not responded. "Please forgive me, my dear man. I could not make out what you were saying over the noise. Could you repeat it for me?"

His companion was only too happy to do so, accepting his explanation without question. Thomas breathed a sigh of relief. He hazarded another glance at Mary and frowned when she smiled at something Mr. Simmons said.

He was still frowning as he answered the gentleman's question, because now she was laughing outright. This was not good. Not good at all.

He did not want Mary to like Mr. Simmons and he certainly did not want her to find him amusing. The man probably possessed the smooth tongue and ease of manner that Thomas always seemed to lack. He wished futilely that he could eavesdrop on what was being said, but he was already impugning all sorts of bad motives on Mr. Simmons just from the smile he was gracing Mary with. Not that there was anything wrong with his smile, per say, but Thomas was sure the man was up to no good. He was a rake, a scoundrel, beyond the shadow of a doubt.

Thomas was suddenly appalled by his line of thought. Why, not long ago, he himself had been gazing at Mary in much the same manner! And if Mr. Simmons had not arrived on the scene, he probably still would be! Thomas was no rake or scoundrel, and it stood to reason that Mr. Simmons was not either.

Thomas turned away from the dance floor and strove to focus his attention on the man beside him, heartily ashamed of himself. He resolved to think no more of Mr. Simmons and Miss Bennet until the time came to claim his dances.

At least *here* there was some comfort. Thomas had already secured her hand for the supper dances, and thereafter the meal. Mr. Simmons could not ruin this source of pleasure for him.

He bided his time until the supper dances came around. Although gentlemen were few, and the ladies many, he chose to remain on the sidelines until his opportunity arose. He was under no false pretenses that the ladies present would desire his hand anyway. There was only one lady for him, and while she did not dance every dance, she was still much sought after, especially once Mr. Simmons had graced her with his attention.

If nothing else, the people of Meryton were innately curious, and having danced with Mr. Simmons, Mary was now a veritable fount of knowledge for them.

She was almost completely worn out by the time Thomas came to claim her hand for the supper dances, having spent a large part of the evening on the dance floor. She was not used to such exertions, having been accustomed to sitting out much of the night on the sidelines, attending to her mother.

Mercifully, Thomas seemed to recognize this, and instead of pressing her to dance, he was content to sit with her and converse.

"I do believe you have become the talk of the assembly," he told her with some humor.

Mary was sorely tempted to roll her eyes. "One set is hardly worthy of so much interest."

"Perhaps not, but Mr. Simmons is, and therefore you must be as well. He has not danced with any lady outside of his own party, with the notable exception of seeking your hand."

"I cannot fathom why. Perhaps he did not wish to excite more gossip by dancing with some other, more beautiful girl."

Thomas could easily fathom why Mr. Simmons would find Mary so appealing, but held his tongue. This was neither the time nor the place for such confessions. Instead, he said, "He would have done better to dispel the gossip by instead dancing with every young lady in attendance."

Mary nodded. "Yes, but at the cost of neglecting his own party. It would be most tiresome, I think, to be constantly introduced and making someone's acquaintance all night long. I know I should not like it."

Thomas was surprised by her response and insight. "You are correct, of course. I, too, would find that wearisome."

She smiled at him in perfect understanding. He longed to reach over and take the hand that rested in her lap. He sighed, finding the restrictions of society cumbersome at that moment.

Mary sought a topic that would interest them both and lit almost instantly upon one. "How were the children this evening? They seemed to be settling down by the time I left this afternoon."

Thomas nodded. "I believe they were worn out from playing in the gardens with Duke. Sophia very nearly fell asleep over tea."

Thus, they embarked on such a mutually agreeable discussion of those so close to their own hearts that it lasted until supper was announced.

Thomas was only too happy to escort Mary in to dine and to find her a spot at an intimate table in the corner. Unfortunately, Lydia flopped into one of the remaining seats, interrupting what would have been a lovely tête-à-tête.

"La! How tired I am!" Lydia exclaimed, fanning herself as her partner and Thomas went off to the buffet. "I danced every dance." She giggled. "The officers have been *very* attentive."

Mary did not doubt this, as Lydia's escort was eyeing her hungrily over his shoulder as he walked, nearly causing him to run into another guest. Lydia giggled and blew him a kiss, and this time he did trip, stumbling into Mrs. Long and spilling her wine on to Mr. Long.

Mary looked away hurriedly as he stumbled through his apologies and focused her attention back on her sister. "Lydia!" she hissed. "You are a married woman! It is unseemly for you to carry on so."

Lydia waved away Mary's concerns. "Lord, what a prude you are! It is just a little harmless flirtation."

"What might seem harmless to you could be very hurtful to others."

Lydia eyed her skeptically, and then flicked her fan shut with a snap. "I suppose you are concerned that I will harm your chances with Mr. Simmons. If you must know, I have no intention of dancing with *him*. What a bore! You two deserve each other." Then she giggled. "Although I certainly would not mind his eight thousand a year!"

Mary could tell her sister was already conjuring up images of carriages and gowns in her mind. "There is more to the man than his money, you know."

Lydia sighed. "When you are made to suffer like I am and live on a pittance, then I give you leave to moralize over me, Mary. But until then, don't tell me there is more to a man than money. I shall not believe you."

"If only you had come to that conclusion before you married Mr. Wickham," Mary muttered darkly. "Then we might all have been spared."

Mary was tired of being embarrassed and ashamed by her sister's antics. She could not stand idly by and allow Lydia to ruin what could be a promising future for her with Thomas by her lack of propriety.

Her statement had the intended effect on her sister. Lydia's lips pressed together into a firm line. Mary recognized the fire that flashed in her eyes and braced herself for an onslaught.

Fortunately for her, Thomas returned at that moment with their plates. "I hope my selections are palatable to you."

She took his offering eagerly. "I am sure whatever you have chosen will be satisfactory."

Thomas seated himself beside her and noticed Lydia watching them with an evil glint in her eye. He shifted uncomfortably under her glare and tried to concentrate on his food. He was not sure what had happened between the sisters while he had been gone, but apparently it had not been pretty.

Lydia seized the opportunity to get back at her sister. She leaned forward and twirled a lock of hair around her finger flirtatiously. "Mr. Bowen, how kind of you to be so solicitous of my sister," she cooed, batting her eyes at him.

Thomas was quickly becoming quite uncomfortable under her attentions. He glanced at Mary out of the corner of his eye, but her head was down and she gave no sign that she had heard her sister. In lieu of understanding what was really going on, he resorted to his usual response in such situations. "Are you aware that the word solicitous comes from the Latin *sollicitus*, which means restless, uneasy, careful, or anxious?"

Thomas could see the boredom overcome her, but still she forced a smile to her lips and pressed on. "How fascinating. You are uncommonly well informed, Mr. Bowen."

"I like to think I am, to a reasonable extent. I believe in bettering myself through education. I would not be setting a good example for my sister's children if I did not."

"I do so admire a man that believes in bettering himself."

Thomas noted with relief the return of Lydia's partner from the buffet. "And what about you, Mrs. Wickham? Do you consider yourself well-informed?"

"In the things that matter," she said coyly. Mary snorted derisively, but by this time Lydia's escort had reached them. He plunked down her plate in front of her and slid into the remaining seat at the table.

"Well, I would say that was an eventful trip to the buffet," he announced. "I am not sure Mrs. Long will ever forgive me for ruining Mr. Long's best coat."

Thomas and Mary looked at each other. Thomas noticed the tiniest hint of a smirk turning up the corners of her mouth. He looked down at his plate in an attempt to hide the grin threatening to overcome his face.

"It is notoriously difficult to recover from the loss of one's best coat," Thomas commented, tongue-in-cheek. "One must find the perfect cut, color, and fit. It is almost impossible to replicate."

Lydia took him seriously. "He will have to apply to the best tailors in London and even then, he may never find exactly the same cut." She giggled. "Not that he should. He looks dreadful in that coat."

Her gentleman companion agreed, laughing along with her. They thus embarked on a long and amiable discussion of the fashion faux pas committed by the vast majority of the assembly at large, leaving Thomas and Mary uncomfortable.

The end of the meal could not come soon enough. The evening that had begun with such promise was now decidedly ruined. Thomas could not engage Mary for any further dances without sparking a great deal of gossip, and Mary could not sit on the sidelines for the rest of the evening and ignore all other partners. When the dancing drew to a close and they all departed, they were both disappointed by the evening.

Mrs. Bennet was all aflutter over what she termed "Mary's greatest success," in securing Mr. Simmons' attentions, but Mary could only deem the night an unmitigated failure, for she had rather hoped for a different gentleman's attentions. And while that gentleman had, in fact, been attentive, their time together had had a pall cast over it by Lydia's interference and blatant flirting.

CHAPTER ELEVEN

Despite the disappointing assembly the evening prior, Mary woke up the next morning still hopeful that all would be well. The day would be rife with opportunities to spend time with Thomas. She could count on him to join them in the gardens after their luncheon and it was quite possible she would see him in the hall as she arrived. And she had even greater reason to believe his presence would be required in the school room that morning, for it was to be Duke's inaugural day in the house.

She dressed quickly, eager to be out of the house before Lydia woke, and even more eager to be at Kaverstow before Duke made his debut. She did not want to miss such a momentous occasion for the children.

She did not bother asking for the carriage, aware that it was most likely needed in the fields. Moreover, she had no desire to be held up by her father and the questions he was sure to pepper her with. He might not have the interest in seeing her married to Mr. Simmons that her mother had, but he was sure to have some clever comment on the situation.

Mary was out the door before anyone in the household, with the exception of the servants, even knew she was awake. She munched on a muffin she had pilfered from the kitchen as she walked, content with her peaceful surroundings.

It was a beautiful morning, full of sunshine, with winter's chill driven almost completely from the air. The birds were singing and flitting cheerfully about, searching for grubs and worms to feed their young.

Mary had never been a great walker, but she could see now why Lizzy had always taken such pleasure in the occupation. On a beautiful spring morning such as this one, there was little that could surpass the pleasure. But Mary knew the pleasure that awaited her at Kaverstow and so quickened her pace, hurrying on to the children and Thomas.

John, Emilia, and Sophia were watching for her from their window in the nursery.

"You don't think she will be late, do you?" Sophia asked worriedly.

"Of course not," said Emilia. "She knows how important today is for us."

John shook his head cynically. "She might know it, but Uncle Thomas came home really late last night from the assembly. I would not be surprised if she doesn't show up until after luncheon."

Sophia pouted, her lower lip jutting out. "But Duke cannot come upstairs without Miss Bennet. It just wouldn't be right. She helped us get his bed together and everything." She gestured to the pile of blankets in one corner.

Emilia patted her little sister's shoulder reassuringly, all the while glaring at her brother over Sophia's head. "Miss Bennet would not forget about us or Duke. She cares about us."

Sophia brightened. "She does, doesn't she?" She turned her attention back to the window, going up on her tiptoes to see out better. "I bet she is right on time, just like she always is."

John snorted at what he deemed to be wishful thinking. Emilia shot him a warning glance at the noise and he turned back to continue watching from the window with a sigh. It was not worth getting his sisters upset over. And indeed, when Mary showed up not just on time, but early, he was immediately repentant for his cynical attitude.

But Sophia still stuck her tongue out at him as she headed out the door to spy on Mary as she came in. As was their habit, he followed his sisters out the door and they snuck down to the landing, peeking through the railing as Bertram greeted Miss Bennet.

And as was his custom, Thomas appeared in the hallway immediately thereafter. "Miss Bennet! I am pleasantly surprised to find you here so early! I hope you are fully recovered from last night's activities?"

Mary was a little taken aback by such a formal greeting, but assured him that she was, in fact, quite recovered, and that she had hastened over in order to be present for Duke's relocation.

Thomas grinned at her, set at ease by her perfectly natural manner. "Ah, yes. I do believe the children are looking forward to it with a great deal of anticipation."

Mary smiled back at him, relieved to see the Thomas she knew reappearing. "I am sure. It is all they have been speaking of for the past two weeks. Have you decided when the deed is to be done?"

Thomas rocked back on his heels. "I had thought to have him brought out to the gardens this afternoon. Then, after everyone has had some time to work out their energy he could come inside with the children."

Mary nodded. "I believe that is an auspicious plan."

Above them, the children were dissatisfied.

"How disappointing," John complained. "I thought they'd bring him in this morning."

Sophia's lower lip started to tremble. "Me, too. He's such a good dog."

John was horrified by the threatening tears. He reached over to pat her shoulder awkwardly. "There, there. It will be alright. Uncle Thomas and Miss Bennet probably just want us to be able to concentrate on our studies this morning."

Emilia hastened to agree with him. "Of course that's the reason! You have to admit, Sophia, that it would be very distracting if Duke was with us."

"You are probably right," Sophia said, sniffling back her tears. "I would want to pet him and hold him and snuggle him instead of working on my embroidery."

"Miss Bennet would certainly not like that," John said. "Her whole job is to teach you things like embroidery and painting tables. Uncle Thomas would be mad at her if she wasn't able to do her job. You wouldn't want to get Miss Bennet in trouble with Uncle Thomas, would you?"

"No," Sophia said indignantly. "But I do wish Duke could come inside sooner."

"I know," soothed Emilia. "We all do. But we will just have to be grateful for the time we do have with him. And after this afternoon, he can be inside almost all the time!"

"And then I'll be able to cuddle with him whenever I want!"

The older siblings exchanged an amused glance. "Yes, Sophia," Emilia said. "As long as we obey Uncle Thomas' rules."

A quick glance down revealed that Miss Bennet was on the verge of coming upstairs, so the girls hastened back to the nursery while John made his presence known to his uncle.

*****

The day progressed in its usual manner, but right before luncheon was to occur, Thomas was surprised by the arrival of an unexpected visitor.

"Mr. Simmons!" Thomas exclaimed in some surprise as the man was shown into his study. They exchanged bows. "Please, take a seat. To what do I owe this pleasure?"

John was quite forgotten in his seat by the fire as Mr. Simmons seated himself across from Thomas.

The other gentleman smiled, perfectly at ease in the foreign environment. "It is rather unorthodox of me to call first, is it not? But I ran across some issues that concern us both as I rode the bounds of my property this morning, and I could not resist the inclination to bring them to your attention. I hope I have not called at an inconvenient time."

"No, not in the least. What has caused you such concern?"

It turned out the flooding that had destroyed his fence line had also done quite a lot of damage to Netherfield's lands. Mr. Simmons was relieved to know that Thomas was already well aware of the problem and had taken steps to repair the damage on his side, but he was keen to discuss solutions to preventing the flooding to begin with.

Eventually, Thomas remembered John and noticed he was listening with rapt attention to the discussion. Anxious to provide the boy with an object lesson for his future use, he called John over to be introduced to Mr. Simmons and included in the conversation.

Together they discussed various ideas and methods that could be used to lower their risk of flooding, but Thomas worried that any measures they might take would have little overall effect. They had no control over any changes upstream and could only hope that what alterations they made on their own properties would be sufficient to control the damage.

Mr. Simmons agreed with the validity of his concerns, but asserted that any changes made could only be for the better. He believed in being proactive. When the visit was over, Thomas found himself with a newfound respect for the man.

He offered to see him out, taking John along with him, as it was the appointed hour for their excursion into the gardens.

Mary descended the stairs with Emilia and Sophia in tow while they were waiting for Bertram to return with Mr. Simmons' gloves and hat.

Both gentlemen turned to look at her, smiling, as she came down the stairs.

"Miss Bennet," Mr. Simmons said, bowing over her hand, "What a delight it is to see you again so soon."

"Likewise, I am sure, Mr. Simmons," Mary said congenially as she curtsied.

The children exchanged worried glances. Mr. Simmons' gaze never left Mary as he collected his things from Bertram.

Thomas noticed as well, and scowled as he tried to hurry the man out the door. "I appreciate your stopping by, Mr. Simmons, and bringing these matters to my attention. I will be sure to call upon you in the near future to discuss them further."

Mr. Simmons finally tore his eyes away from Mary. "Yes, yes, of course. Anytime." They shook hands and Mr. Simmons allowed himself to be ushered outside to his waiting carriage.

"What did Mr. Simmons want to discuss?" asked Mary as they all stood outside, watching him drive away.

"Nothing to be too concerned about," Thomas answered. "There has been some flooding in some of the fields and he wanted to discuss some ideas for remedying the situation."

"It is a common problem to have in Hertfordshire, is it not?"

"Yes. And not one with an easy solution, or it would have been resolved long ago. He is an ambitious man, and not one to sit about quietly doing nothing. I will give him that much."

Mary smiled at him. "Much like you in that respect, I should think."

Thomas was touched by the compliment. "I should like to think so." He smiled down at her and touched her hand briefly with his own to express his thanks. He longed to intertwine his fingers with hers, but instead he cleared his throat and said, "Shall we go down into the gardens? I think there is a certain puppy that should very much like to see everyone."

His purposefully light tone had the children running ahead, all concerns forgotten for the moment. He snuck glances at Mary as they walked, but she had her head down and her eyes on the path.

He wished he could know what she was thinking, with the sudden appearance of Mr. Simmons at Kaverstow. Still, he was cheered by her reaction to his presence. She had been polite but cool, unlike her gentle familiarity with Thomas. He liked to think their relationship meant more to her than that of just an employer and employee, and that his friendship was more valuable to her than that of a wealthy acquaintance.

If only he could be sure that it was more than mere friendship between them. But he had no such confirmation, as Mary was all that was proper in all but the most extraordinary of circumstances, and he could hardly base their relationship on those few and far between instances.

Thomas had insisted that Duke be brought out before the children came down, and so it was that by the time he and Mary joined them in the gardens, the space was already filled with laughter and squeals of delight.

He smiled broadly to see the children so happy, and Mary wound her arm through his and squeezed it with joy.

"Oh, look how happy they are!" she exclaimed. She laughed as the puppy jumped on Sophia, knocking her over so he could excitedly lick her in the face. "And he is undoubtedly just as pleased to see them." She turned her laughing face up to Thomas and pressed a chaste kiss to his cheek without thinking. "You were right to give them this."

He would have kissed her then, the instinct overwhelming all rational thought, but she let go of his arm and hurried over to join the children in their frenzy of excitement.

Shocked by the direction his thoughts, and almost his actions, had taken, Thomas hung back.

Her kiss burned his cheek. He could still feel clearly the imprint of her lips on his skin and his fingers itched to touch the spot, not to rub away the sensation, but to seal it in, to reassure himself that it had been real.

He was astounded by the simple gesture, but unsure how to take it. What had she meant by the salute? Was it simply a gesture between friends, or did it signify something deeper, something more? His mind whirled with endless possibilities.

He needed to proceed with caution, he decided. It was possible her kiss meant everything he hoped it did, but there was the distinct possibility it did not, that it had only arose from the emotion of the moment. He would have to be careful to keep his feelings hidden until he had the opportunity to discover hers.

With this new resolve, he went forward to join the mayhem.

CHAPTER TWELVE

Mary laid her head back against the tree trunk she was resting against and savored the feel of the breeze on her face and the calm in the air. It was a rare day off, Thomas having informed her that he was expecting a visitor that day and would have no need of her services.

She was unexpectedly lonely, even with Longbourn full and her Mamma and Lydia at home. There were no children to hug or injuries to kiss better. No one here needed, or for that matter, desired, her expertise or opinions. She missed that unexpected pleasure she had found at Kaverstow, of her company and thoughts being desired. But most of all, she missed Thomas and their daily interaction.

He had become such an integral part of her life so quickly. Now her day just did not feel complete without seeing him or speaking to him. She sighed wistfully and wondered where he was at that moment and what he was doing.

The frantic calling of her name drew her attention toward the house and brought a furrow to her brow.

Hill was rushing towards her, waving madly. "Miss Bennet! Miss Bennet!"

Mary gathered her things in alarm and rose to meet her halfway down the hill. "What is it, Hill? Is everything all right? Has Mamma had another of her spells?"

The other woman paused to catch her breath after fairly racing across the lawn. "Your Mamma told me to fetch you with all haste. You are needed in the parlor."

"Of course." Mary could not imagine what could have happened to necessitate such haste, but it must have been something of grave importance for her mother to concern herself with it. "I shall go at once." Without waiting for the housekeeper to respond, she set off towards the house at a brisk pace.

She did not pause to remove her bonnet or gloves, instead going straight into the parlor, stripping off her gloves as she went. "What is it, Ma-"

She froze as she realized her mother was not the only person in the room.

Mrs. Bennet rose to greet her, beaming from ear to ear and winking conspiratorially. "Why there you are, Mary! I was just telling Mr. Simmons that I was sure you would be in directly. Did I not, Mr. Simmons?"

Mr. Simmons came to bow over her hand. "You most certainly did, Mrs. Bennet. It is a pleasure to see you again, Miss Bennet."

He lingered a little longer than necessary over her hand and Mary quickly snatched it back from his possession at the first inclination of a lessening in his grip. "Likewise, I am sure."

Lydia covered up a giggle with a cough from her spot in the corner and Mary was hard pressed to ignore her. She struggled to gather her wits back about her after being caught so off-guard. "If you will just excuse me for a moment, I shall be back down shortly to receive you properly." She made her curtsey and beat a hasty retreat from the room, her mind whirring.

Whatever could her mother be thinking? She yanked her fingers through the ribbons of her bonnet as she tore up the stairs to her room. The woman must be mad!

Even if the man did have some genuine interest in her, which she sincerely doubted, given the circumstances, her mother's scheming was sure to scare him off. The poor man and his eight thousand a year were better off within the safe confines of Netherfield, for both their sakes; for Mary was just as surely as uninterested in him as he was in her. She just wished there was some easy way to absolve herself from her mother's machinations.

She lobbed her bonnet on to the bed, her gloves quickly following them. Within moments she had divested herself of her outerwear and was changing out of her morning dress into something more appropriate to receive callers in.

Only a few minutes later, she was tidying up her hair and checking her appearance in the mirror. There was no need to pinch color into her cheeks, for her mother's antics had already stained them pink. Satisfied that she was suitably attired to receive their guest, she took a deep breath and descended the stairs with a pretended calm she could not possess.

She pasted a gracious smile on her face and let herself into the parlor. She was immediately greeted by its occupants and forced to take a seat and have an active part in the conversation, as lackluster as it was.

Her mother was droning on about Mary's accomplishments in great detail, with nary a pause for anyone to get a word in edgewise. Mary pretended great interest in her mother's words, while secretly scheming of ways to escape the dull rigors of the parlor. She nodded along at all the appropriate points, keeping one eye on the door and any excuse to exit through it.

Mr. Simmons seemed to notice her preoccupation and cut her mother off in the middle of a sentence. "I have heard so much of your accomplishments, Miss Bennet, especially at the pianoforte. Perhaps you might play for us?"

Mrs. Bennet was pleased with his suggestion, and gestured with little shooing motions for Mary to do as he asked. "It is the very thing, Mr. Simmons. The very thing! I could not have suggested better myself! My dear Mary, do play for us!"

Mary reluctantly pried herself from her chair and crossed the room to the pianoforte, which was even farther from the door and any potential escape.

"My Mary plays so beautifully, Mr. Simmons! You shall not be disappointed, I daresay."

Mr. Simmons only looked mildly amused by Mrs. Bennet's enthusiastic response.

Lydia rolled her eyes and snorted. "I daresay, indeed."

Mary ignored her sarcastic comment and rifled through the sheet music for something suitable to play.

Many of the heavy, difficult pieces she generally preferred would be inappropriate candidates for what she hoped would be a short display of her prowess at the pianoforte. She finally found a suitable piece and set about playing with all the skill she possessed.

Mr. Simmons listened attentively while she played and applauded with great gusto at the conclusion of the piece. "Brava! Brava! Very nicely done, Miss Bennet!"

Mary took his words with a grain of salt, believing him to be only being polite. She dropped a curtsey and then moved to join the group before she could be applied to to play again.

Mary was relieved when Mr. Simmons excused himself shortly thereafter, the polite length of time for a visit having been long up. But Mrs. Bennet could not let him escape without extending and securing his acceptance of an invitation to dine with them later in the week.

"Do say you will join us, Mr. Simmons, for a family dinner? It shall be at least three courses."

Mr. Simmons glanced at Mary and then back to her mother. "I shall be delighted to accept." He bowed and left them, following Hill out.

Mary stood to excuse herself after the door had closed behind him, but Mrs. Bennet immediately launched into raptures, delaying her strategic exit.

Mrs. Bennet scurried across the room to squeeze Mary's cheeks. "Oh my dear, dear, Mary! My sweet, wonderful Mary! You are saved at last!"

Mary tried to pry her face free from her mother's relentless grasp, and failed miserably. "Mamma! You are hurting me!"

Lydia snorted. "I would hardly say she is saved yet, Mamma. Even if Mr. Simmons *is* showing an inordinate amount of interest in her, he has not yet made her an offer. He is probably just looking for a little country nobody to amuse himself with before he goes back to Town."

Mrs. Bennet rounded on Lydia with surprising venom. "Hush child! That comment smacks strongly of jealousy! I will not have you dashing your sister's chances with Mr. Simmons!"

Both Lydia and Mary were taken aback by this surprising reversal of roles. There was a pregnant pause as everyone in the room was startled into silence.

Then Lydia's lower lip started to extrude into a pout as the barest hint of a smile played around Mary's lips.

"How can you say such a thing, Mamma, when you know how little I have and how much my sisters have?" Lydia's lower lip started to quiver, and Mrs. Bennet was instantly repentant, fairly flying across the room to comfort her favorite.

"There, there, dear. I did not mean it like that." Mrs. Bennet wrapped her arms around her youngest daughter and patted her on the back.

The smile disappeared from Mary's lips.

"Besides, why should I be jealous of Mary?" Lydia sniffed. "*I* have got a husband, and he is *ever* so much more handsome than Mr. Simmons."

"You are right, dear," Mrs. Bennet soothed. "Mr. Wickham is quite handsome and charming, but Mr. Simmons is handsome in his own right, I daresay."

Lydia frowned over her mother's shoulder. "But not as handsome as my Wickham."

"Of course not, dear. Mr. Wickham is especially handsome by all means. And that red coat! Why, if I were a young woman I would be tempted to engage in a little harmless flirtation myself!"

Lydia giggled, and Mary shook her head in amazement at her sister's manipulative ways. She took the opportunity to slip out into the hall while her mother was otherwise occupied. Mrs. Bennet would never even suspect how easily Lydia had played her.

She felt a sudden desire to escape the clutches of her family. Without hesitation, she donned the garb she had so hastily discarded earlier and retreated outside, walking quickly in an effort to travel far out of the reach of her family's grasp.

She walked without a destination in mind, but soon found her feet carrying her in the direction of a local landmark, Oakham Mount. When she realized where she was headed, she smiled. It had been a long time since she had ventured so far, but the view held an appeal she could not resist. Her family would never think to look for her there.

The climb was a little tiring for someone unused to such distances, but the view from the top was well worth it. Mary took a deep breath of the fresh, clean, crisp air and smiled as the breeze teased tendrils of her hair free from her bonnet.

She stood there for several minutes, just enjoying the scenery, before the sound of someone clearing their throat behind her drew her attention.

Her initial alarm at the sound was quickly replaced with delight when she turned around and saw who stood behind her. "Why, Thomas, I did not expect to see you here!"

Thomas came forward out of the shadows. He had been seated on a fallen log when Mary had appeared before him. He took the hand she happily held out to him and bowed over it. "Nor I you."

"But should you not be at home? Was your guest delayed?"

Thomas shook his head. "No. He arrived exactly as he had stated."

Mary cocked her head and looked at him questioningly. His tone was despairing and he was uncharacteristically subdued.

Thomas recognized her look of concern. He sighed and tugged her back to his makeshift bench. "Come, sit here beside me. I shall tell you all about it, for it concerns you as well, I am afraid."

She obliged him, settling on to the fallen tree without a thought for her clothing. Her concern and attention were fully caught up in the man before her. What could have gone so horribly wrong, so quickly?

Thomas sat beside her, still clutching her hand, grasping at the security she offered while his whole world was tumbling down around him.

"Do you remember that the children's father was at sea when my sister died?"

Mary nodded mutely.

Thomas sighed. "Well, he has returned."

Mary opened her mouth to respond, but then closed it again, absorbing this piece of information. Finally, she said slowly, "Is he your guest? Their father?"

Thomas nodded. "I thought it best to allow him some time alone with his children." He raked his fingers through his hair and let out his breath is a noisy rush. "And I desperately needed some time alone to think." He turned to face Mary, speaking earnestly. "He told me this morning he is thinking of taking them back to Portsmouth when he leaves."

Mary blinked and fought to quell the emotions that rose in her. "Oh." When she could think somewhat rationally, she said, "But what of when he is at sea? Surely he would not leave them alone?"

Thomas sighed heavily. "He spoke of hiring someone to care for them while he is away."

Mary bit her tongue to keep herself from saying what she really thought of that idea, but Thomas gave her a knowing look. She was not thinking anything he had not already thought. She gave him a small smile and he smiled grimly back, his hold tightening on her hand.

"I know I have complained about them," Thomas said, "But now that I am faced with losing them, I cannot contemplate my life without them. Kaverstow would be so *empty*."

"Have you informed the children's father of how you feel? Perhaps he is only considering removing them because he fears you must view the children as a burden."

"I have not forced the issue yet," Thomas admitted. "He has only just arrived. For all I know, the children might prefer that arrangement. I could not stand in the way if it is truly better for them."

"Do you truly believe returning to Portsmouth is in their best interests?"

"No. I do not. Their father is gone for months at a time. No housekeeper would care for them as I do while he is away. But in the end, I am not their father, and I have no right to make that decision for him."

Mary had no choice but to agree with his reasoning. "I still think you should speak to him and make it plain that you are perfectly happy with continuing as things are."

Thomas squeezed her hand. "I shall, I promise." He sought to change the topic to a happier one. "What brought you so far from home this day?"

Mary made a face. "Mamma and Lydia were making a nuisance of themselves. I needed to get away."

Thomas cocked his head. "In what way?"

Mary sighed. She really did not want to go into it, as the situation did not reflect well on her or her family. She tried to gloss over all that had happened. "Mr. Simmons called at Longbourn this afternoon and Mamma was quite in dithers over it."

Thomas' hand tightened possessively on hers at the mention of Mr. Simmons. He scowled. What was that man doing calling at Longbourn on *his* Mary?

Mary did not fail to notice the change that came over his countenance. She looked at him wonderingly, curious as to what Mr. Simmons had done to incur his dislike. The two men had seemed to get along just fine when she had encountered them together at Kaverstow.

Thomas hastened to speak before she could question him about his reaction. "And what of Mrs. Wickham? Surely, she would not have reacted in the same way as your mother to Mr. Simmons?"

Mary shook her head and turned away to gaze at the view. "No, her complaints were of a different nature."

Thomas turned her head gently so that her gaze once more met his own, tender one. "What were her complaints?"

Mary blushed but did not pull away from his touch. "It does not signify."

Thomas raised one brow, daring to disagree with her assessment without openly challenging her statement. Whatever she might claim to the contrary, he knew that Mrs. Wickham's complaints did, in fact, signify to Mary. Mrs. Wickham probably never thought twice about how her words would affect Mary, but it was evident to him that they had stung. Otherwise, Mary would never have sought refuge so far from home. She was not one to roam the countryside on her own, preferring to stick closer to the safety of home.

Mary's blush deepened at his knowing look and she pulled away from him. Thomas let her go, reluctantly. It was not his place to force her to confront her familial issues. At least not yet.

He let the silence lengthen between them, content for the moment to just sit with her at his side and enjoy the view.

At length, Mary began to fidget beside him. He turned to her with a smile. "Are you ready to return?"

She nodded and smiled at his understanding.

He stood and held his hand out to help her off the fallen log. "Come. I will escort you home."

She did not attempt to dissuade him. Instead, she took his hand and allowed him to pull her up. And if she just happened to fail to release his hand once she was on her feet, well, neither of them was complaining.

"I feel it is only fair to warn you that the children may be especially excitable tomorrow," Thomas commented as they walked. "I am not sure just how their routine will be thrown off by their father's arrival, but I feel it prudent to try to keep them to as much of their normal schedule as possible."

Mary agreed. "I think that is wise."

"I will probably be sending you John in the morning to care for while I speak with his father. I hope that is not too much of an imposition."

"I will not find it so, but John may be disgruntled to be relegated back to the nursery with his sisters."

"He may very well be," Thomas admitted. "But it is a necessary evil, and he needs to learn how to handle disappointments. There are liable to be more before this visit is over." He offered her a lop-sided grin. "Even for me."

"How did the children react to their father's arrival?" Mary asked. "Did they know he was coming?"

Thomas shook his head. "I thought it better not to raise their hopes, only to have them disappointed if he had been unable to come."

"I am sure they were pleased."

"Very much so. They were very eager to show Duke off to him as well."

"If they did return to Portsmouth, would they be able to keep Duke?"

Thomas shrugged. "I do not know. The decision is not mine. But I can tell you that it would be a difficult adjustment for him to make to go from the freedom of the countryside to the crapped confines of town."

"It is certainly something to consider. I know the children would be heartbroken to leave him behind. He is of great comfort to them, and would continue to be so should they return. Especially with their father at sea for so long a time." She paused before saying sadly, "I should hate to see them go."

Thomas smiled at her. "I know. I should, too."

"I do hope you shall be able to change his mind," Mary said earnestly.

"I shall do my best."

They were nearing Longbourn. The lane that led to Mary's home appeared out of the underbrush. Thomas drew her to a halt. "I will leave you here. I shall see you in the morning?"

Mary smiled. "Of course."

Thomas searched her eyes, desperately seeking some reassurance that this constant in his life, her presence, was not going to change as well. The urge to kiss her, to claim her as his own for all time, was overwhelming.

But he could not ask that impropriety of her, not when he knew they were both distressed by the thought of losing the children. It would be the act of a moment, built on their possible loss, not out of a shared love.

Instead, he released her hand and watched her walk away, pausing at the turn to Longbourn to wave good-bye. He waved back and, when she had disappeared from view, turned to start his own journey home, squaring his shoulders against the turmoil that awaited him there.

CHAPTER THIRTEEN

Mary did not know what awaited her when she arrived at Kaverstow the next morning. She dreaded the possibility of bad news, while desperately hoping for good. She received neither.

Instead, she entered the house to find three children wild with excitement and eager to introduce her to their father. Fortunately for her, their father was already holed up with Thomas in his study, sparing her what could have been a very awkward interview. She would have to be introduced to the man eventually, but she hoped when it did occur it would be on more adult terms than what she suspected the children had in mind.

Unfortunately, that still left her with three rambunctious children that had absolutely no intention of settling down to their schoolwork. Mary still felt it her duty to try, but she was wise enough to employ a change in tactics.

"I believe we shall have our lessons in the garden today," she suggested. "Girls, please fetch your samplers." She sent them scurrying up the steps.

John waited patiently for her to instruct him, but when she remained silent, he finally spoke up. "Should I bring anything, Miss Bennet?"

She shook her head. "No, John. The samplers are only for just in case. I have a few other activities in mind for all of you."

The girls came running back down, and Mary took them each by the hand, leading her little gaggle outside, Duke following behind them. She had the girls leave their samplers on a bench by the house, where they would be safe, and directed them down a nearby path. "I thought we might have a lesson in horticulture this morning."

"What is horticulture?" asked Sophia, stumbling over the unfamiliar word.

"Can anyone else explain what horticulture is?" asked Mary.

John frowned. "Is it like farming?"

"Similar," Mary said. "It does have to do with cultivating plants. What do you think, Emilia?"

"Is it cultivating flowers?"

"That is part of it. Horticulture is the art of cultivating flowers, fruits, vegetables, or ornamental plants. Who do we know that does all those things?"

The children chimed triumphantly, "The gardener!"

Mary smiled. "So who do you think we should talk to in order to learn about horticulture?"

"Mr. Walker?" asked John.

"He is the head gardener, is he not?"

"Yes."

"Then that is who we are going to see," said Mary. "And I happen to know that Mr. Walker is overseeing the weeding of the daffodils today." She pointed him out as the path they were on dipped and the daffodils came into view.

She shooed the children on to run ahead, and they were already peppering Mr. Walker with questions when she drew abreast of them. She smiled at the success of her cunning plan, even as Mr. Walker was overwhelmed by his sudden companions and shot her a disgruntled look. She gave him a sunny smile and was rewarded for her efforts when he smiled back begrudgingly.

They spent most of the morning following Mr. Walker about as he attended to his various duties and assisting him as they could. Mary was pleased with the children's efforts, and pleased at the opportunity to increase their understanding of all the work that went into keeping their home maintained.

When it was time for luncheon to be served, they waved good-bye to their new friend and headed back to the house. The meal had been set out on the terrace. The children were famished after the morning's activities and needed no coaxing from Mary to fill their plates and sit down to eat.

When they had finished, Mary suggested bird watching on the lawn, and that was how Thomas found them when he came upon them sometime later. They were sprawled on a blanket on the lawn, laying on their backs and pointing out the different birds that flew overhead.

He grinned at the casual picture they presented. What he would not give to have them like this every day! It would be a pleasure to have Mary so relaxed and comfortable at Kaverstow, and to have her truly view it as her home.

He wanted it to be her home. He wanted her to be mistress over it all. But he lacked the courage to ask when she would have every right to refuse him.

He could not make her an offer that would compare to what Mr. Simmons could give her and he could not ask her to give up the comforts she might have and the distance from her family she might desire.

The children's father, John, came to stand beside him and smiled at the sight of his children so at ease. "So this is the illustrious Miss Bennet I have heard so much about?" he asked Thomas, as they were still out of earshot of the group on the lawn.

"It is."

"The children certainly seem taken with her."

"I believe so."

John eyed Thomas knowingly. "They are not the only ones taken with her, I see."

Thomas swung around to face him, shocked by his perception. "Pardon me?!"

John grinned and slapped him on the back. "I would recognize that look anywhere, Thomas. I have worn it myself often enough. You are besotted with Miss Bennet."

Thomas just grunted and turned back to look out over the lawn again, unwilling to admit out loud the truth of the matter. But John did not need any confirmation from him.

"Have you made her an offer?" he asked Thomas.

Thomas shook his head mutely.

"Surely at the very least you have told her how you feel?"

Again, Thomas shook his head. "How can I? She deserves far more than anything I could offer her."

John laughed and clapped him on the shoulder. "No man ever deserves the love of a fine woman, Thomas, but sometimes they are willing to give it anyway. You will never know if you do not ask." He winked and sauntered down the lawn to greet his children and their governess. Thomas watched, pensive, as Mary stood to be introduced and the children clamored to do the honors. The smile she bestowed upon John was welcoming and friendly.

Perhaps his brother-in-law was right, he mused. He owed it to Mary to tell her the truth and then see where his cards lay. But he could not do that until he knew what future he had to offer her, and that all depended on John and whether he decided to leave the children at Kaverstow.

Their discussion that morning had been enlightening, but Thomas was still uncertain of what John intended to do. He had made no final decisions, only mentioning that he would let Thomas know what he had determined before the visit was over.

Thomas sighed and squared his shoulders. There was nothing he could do about the situation now. He started down to join the group below.

*****

Almost a week later, Thomas was beginning to feel like an outsider in his own home. It was Mary's day off, and his brother-in-law, John, had rounded up his children and taken them outside to play.

The house was quiet. Too quiet. Thomas could not think with so much oppressive silence. His gaze kept drifting toward the door, waiting for someone to burst in on him and interrupt his work. He fought the urge to pace by the window and sneak peeks at the children playing below.

He drummed his fingers on his desk. With John's arrival, his role had suddenly been usurped. He did not know how he fit in anymore. He did not want to intrude on the little time the children had with their father, yet he yearned to be in on the action.

Peals of delighted laughter floated in through the open window and he could stand it no longer. He had to get away from Kaverstow. He rang for Bertram and instructed the man to have his carriage brought round.

If he could not rely on the charms of Kaverstow to distract him, he knew someone whose charms would.

*****

The elder John watched Thomas' departure with a smug smile. He had a good idea where his brother was headed, and it pleased him to no end. The man deserved a little happiness in his life. Even if Mary Bennet only brought Thomas a fraction of the joy his Anne had brought him, Thomas would be better for it.

The smile died on his lips at the thought of his late wife. He still had not adjusted to her loss. It had been a shock, to disembark expecting a warm welcome home, only to find an empty house awaiting him. He had been desperate, those first few days, to have his children back around him.

There was so much of Anne in them. He could see her in every smile and laugh, in every stubborn insistence on having their own way, and even in the way they fought for and protected their puppy.

When he was with them, he remembered all the reasons he had to go on, even without her by his side, supporting his every activity.

Unfortunately though, his leave would not last forever, and he was faced with some difficult decisions as to his children's futures. He had come to Kaverstow with every intention of absconding with them upon the conclusion of his visit. They had no place in the care of an uncle they had never even had the opportunity to meet before his wife's untimely death.

Now, he was not so sure that was the best course of action. His children were happy here; happier than he had ever imagined they could be without their mother. They loved Thomas and they adored Miss Bennet. Their uncle could give them a life John could only dream of giving them. They had land to play on and space for Duke. They would not be left in the care of servants for months on end while he traveled, but they would be well taken care of by a family member who loved them. His brother-in-law had made it abundantly clear he had no aversion to them staying.

Thomas was training his son to take over Kaverstow one day, and under Miss Bennet's guidance his daughters would grow up to be the ladies Anne would have wanted them to be. Even if Thomas did marry Miss Bennet and have a son of his own, as John was strongly inclined to believe he would, he knew Thomas would make sure his children were abundantly provided for.

When he did return on leave, they would be right here, waiting for him.

"Pappa, what are you thinking about so hard?" Sophia asked, breaking in on his thoughts.

He mustered up a reassuring smile. "I was just thinking about your Uncle Thomas, dear. Do you like it here with him very much?"

Sophia nodded vigorously. "Oh yes, Pappa! He is ever so nice! He let us keep Duke and he never ever yells, even when we run off and hide from him."

Emilia chimed in, "And Miss Bennet is teaching me how to play the pianoforte. She says I will be a beautiful lady someday. I think Mamma would like that, don't you?"

He smiled tightly, wishing the pressure in his chest that arose at the mention of her mother would go away. "I think she would like that very much." His son had remained silent, so he tried to draw him out. "What about you, John? Do you like it here?"

John hesitated. "Yes, Pappa. Mostly."

"Mostly?"

"Well, sometimes I don't like it when Uncle Thomas tells me what to do."

His father smothered a smile. Of course. How like his mother he was! "You would feel the same way about me though, would you not?"

John shrugged, which his father recognized was his way of admitting that the statement was probably true.

At least their uncle knew he had the authority to tell the children what to do. He was not sure the servants in Portsmouth would have the same confidence. They would be afraid to enforce the rules or punish them in his absence. He had the niggling suspicion that his children would run rough-shod over the household there.

Helene climbed into his lap and settled down to play with the buttons on his coat. He dropped a kiss on her downy head. Even his littlest was well adjusted to life at Kaverstow. He had been pleased with her nursemaid and relieved to see she still spent a large amount of time with her brother and sisters.

Perhaps he had been hasty to suggest packing them all up again and bringing them back to Portsmouth. He was normally a man of quick action, used to making decisions on the fly and trusting his gut, so it was difficult to admit that his first impulse might not be the best decision for his family.

But now he knew what the right choice was.

*****

Thomas handed his hat and gloves to Hill and waited to be introduced before he entered the Bennet's parlor. Butterflies fluttered in his stomach as Mrs. Bennet's high-pitched voice filtered through the walls. He hoped he had done the right thing by coming here. If not, he was about to be trapped in a room with Mrs. Bennet for a quarter hour. The prospect was not appealing.

Hill gestured for him to go in, and he did, his eyes searching for the one face he wanted most to see. His gaze was immediately drawn to Mary. She was seated by the window, where, just moments ago, she had been gazing wistfully out while wishing for his presence. Her smile bloomed at the sight of him and warmth rushed through him at her friendly welcome.

He would have gladly gone to her and never left her side, but a male voice calling his name interrupted his thoughts. He swung his head around and fought to quell the annoyance that flooded through him.

"Mr. Simmons," he said politely, crossing to shake the other man's hand. "I did not expect to find you here."

"Nor I you," Mr. Simmons replied with a genuine smile. "What a pleasant surprise! I was just informing Mrs. Bennet about our little flooding problem and how you have been of much assistance to me with the matter."

Thomas took a seat by the man, unable to see how he could politely extradite himself from the conversation now. "I do not think I have been of much assistance. You seem to have the matter well in hand."

"Oh no! You have been a very valuable aid to me! I was pleased to have a neighbor that has such an active share in his estate dealings."

"As am I."

Lydia and Mrs. Bennet were growing quite bored with this conversation.

"Tell me, Mr. Simmons, of your house in Town," Mrs. Bennet broke in. "Every gentleman of your caliber must have a house in Town. Is it on Grosvenor Square?" She leaned forward eagerly, already mentally redecorating what she was sure was a fine, large townhouse.

Mr. Simmons smiled. "I do not have a house in Town. I find the air intolerable there. I much prefer the fresh breezes of Hertfordshire."

Mrs. Bennet was flabbergasted. All her visions of a fine home in Town where Mary would welcome her with open arms for the Season melted away into a puddle of horror. "No townhouse?! But surely you jest, Mr. Simmons!"

Mr. Simmons was taken aback. "I assure you, I do not, Mrs. Bennet."

"Tell us of your estate, then," Lydia inserted as Mrs. Bennet attempted to collect herself. "Surely, you have a lovely estate?"

Mr. Simmons tried not to smile. "I believe it to be beautiful, indeed, but you must know more about Netherfield as its longstanding neighbors than I do in my short time here."

Mrs. Bennet was on the verge of hyperventilating. No townhouse?! No estate?! How could a man with almost ten thousand a year have no home? Where were her grandchildren going to grow up? Where was Mary to be situated? They would not be forever at Netherfield, would they? A man with nine thousand a year needed a grand home with large attics! Her dreams for Mary were crashing down around her.

Meanwhile, Lydia was smirking. It served Mary right to be stuck in Hertfordshire forever, never being able to enjoy the entertainment of London! She did not deserve a large townhouse and an estate and a box at the theatre, not like Lydia did.

If Lydia could not have those things then she did not want Mary to have them either!

Mary was not unsettled by these revelations. It mattered not to her what possessions Mr. Simmons did or did not have, for she had no intention of them ever becoming hers. Instead, she shared a rueful glance with Thomas at her family's erratic behavior.

He shook his head slightly at her, commiserating, before he turned back to the conversation and tried to steer it into a more productive direction. "Netherfield is a lovely estate, Mr. Simmons. I admit I am a little biased towards Kaverstow, myself, but Netherfield has some beautiful vistas."

Mr. Simmons beamed at his praise of Netherfield. "I could not agree more with you, Mr. Bowen."

Mary rose to join the group, eager to support Thomas. "My sister, Jane, had the pleasure of staying there some years ago. She spoke very highly of the place and its staff."

"Oh, yes, the staff is quite excellent," Mr. Simmons replied. "Of course, I have brought some of my own, more principal, servants with me. But the locals I hired have been very accommodating as well."

"There are many honest, hard-working folk in this area," Mary agreed. "You will not find a more pleasant people in all of England."

Thomas wished he could reach over and squeeze her hand for the support. The bounds of propriety chaffed when he had tasted of the sweetness that lay outside their grasp.

Mr. Simmons turned his smile on Mary, pleased to have her finally playing an active part in the conversation instead of day-dreaming by the window. "That has been my experience as well. Country life is so invigorating. Town may have more diversity, but its charms cannot compare to the country life. Do you agree, Miss Bennet?"

Mary strove to keep her voice level and her eyes off Thomas, as they surely would have given away her feelings if she dared to look at him. "I do. I find I prefer the country life with our quiet ways and intimate associations. I would not enjoy Town."

"I am pleased to know we are so like-minded on the subject." He beamed at her, even as her smile disappeared.

She had not intended her comment to be a reflection on their compatibility. She snuck a glance at her mother, whose dreamy smile revealed that she had heard the same connotation. She dared not look at Thomas.

She shifted uncomfortably in her seat and blurted, "I am sure there are other topics on which we disagree. For instance, I find the study of horticulture to be quite fascinating."

Mr. Simmons was puzzled by the vehemence of her response. "I believe horticulture to be a noble hobby, Miss Bennet. How could it not be, when one is laboring among God's creations?"

Mary pressed her lips together into a firm line and decided it was in her best interests to remain silent. One attempt gone horribly wrong was quite enough. Who knew what further foolishness might spill out if she was to open her mouth again?

Mrs. Bennet spoke up to fill what was becoming an awkward silence while shooting a reproving glance at Mary. "That is just what I always say, Mr. Simmons. Time spent laboring in the garden is well-spent in God's work."

"Indeed, indeed," Mr. Simmons agreed. He rested his hands on his knees and made to stand up. "I thank you for the pleasant visit, Miss Bennet, Mrs. Bennet, and Mrs. Wickham. I believe I must leave you now." He stood and made his bows and at least two of those present watched him leave with unbridled relief.

After the parlor door had closed behind him, Thomas leaned forward to address Mary, a smile playing about his lips. "I should very much like to see these gardens I have heard so much about, Miss Bennet, if your mother can spare you."

Mary grinned back at him. "I believe that can be arranged. They are quite lovely this time of year." They applied to her mother and were granted permission. Now that Mr. Simmons had gone, Mrs. Bennet had no need of Mary in the drawing room when Lydia could entertain her so well, nor did Mary need a chaperone when they would be within sight of the parlor.

They eagerly adjourned to the gardens, which were really very pretty this time of year. Unfortunately, the beauty surrounding them went unnoticed, as, by their very nature, a young couple such as Mary and Thomas had eyes only for each other.

Of course, they were oblivious to this knowledge, neither having the courage nor the audacity to share their heart's desires without first being assured of them being reciprocated.

So, in its place, they spent a very pleasant half hour in the gardens, reveling in the other's company and attention, neither taking the opportunity presented by their solitude.

Mary was eager to ask after the children and inquire as to their father's decision, but Thomas had no news to report on that front and was not willing to present his own conjecture on the subject.

Instead, he inquired after Longbourn's house guest, as it appeared that Mrs. Wickham was inclined to remain indefinitely.

Mary was hard-pressed not to roll her eyes at the mention of Lydia. "My sister does not possess the discernment that would suggest she has overstayed her welcome. And indeed, Mamma is quite fond of her company. Pappa, on the other hand, I believe, finds that her presence only encourages Mamma in her nerves and flights of fancy. He is ready for her to return to her husband and her home, as am I."

"Will your father speak to her?"

Mary shrugged. "I cannot say. Pappa is not one who is inclined to do much unless his own comfort is disturbed. I do not believe Mamma's nerves are enough of an inducement in and of themselves for him to involve himself. But we shall see. Things may very well change."

Thomas smiled wanly, her words reminding him of how much his own little world had changed in the preceding weeks. "How true. We can never know what tomorrow holds for us." He squeezed the hand that rested in the crook of his arm. "Let us hope it brings glad tidings."

Mary could do naught but agree, and so they turned the conversation to happier topics for the remainder of their time in the gardens. The precious time they had together could not be spoiled by the shadows of their guests.

And when Thomas had departed and Mary returned to the parlor, they were both soothed by the fond memories of their time together.

CHAPTER FOURTEEN

Tomorrow, it turned out, did not bring glad tidings to Thomas. Soon after Mary had arrived and disappeared upstairs with the children, he received an unexpected visitor.

Bertram showed a decidedly nervous Mr. Simmons into Thomas' study.

"Mr. Simmons," Thomas said in astonishment, standing to shake his hand. "What a pleasant surprise!"

Mr. Simmons pumped his hand and then started pacing before his desk, words tumbling from his lips. "Yes. It is, is it not? I really had no intention of visiting so soon after having run into you at the Bennet's, but it occurred to me that you could be of the utmost help to me in my current predicament."

Thomas slowly sank back into his seat, overcome with dread, as the man continued.

"I have recently found myself entertaining the thought of taking a wife, and a most suitable young lady has been introduced to me as a prospective match. Surely, you must know of whom I speak. As Miss Bennet's employer you must have some insight into the young lady. Do you suppose she would respond favorably to a marriage proposal?"

Flabbergasted, Thomas could not respond for several moments. Never before had he been placed in such an awkward position. The man before him, blissfully ignorant of his feelings, wanted him to give him his blessing to pursue the woman Thomas himself was in love with!

It was almost more than he could bear. And yet, he could not deny the man his opportunity, nor could he separate Mary from Mr. Simmons, should that be her choice. He certainly had extracted no promise from her that would prevent an understanding from being reached between them. Unfortunately.

He kicked himself now for not seizing their precious moments together to do so. As it was, he had no good reason to dissuade the man, other than his own selfish inclinations.

He chose to be honest. "I regret that I cannot inform you as to that lady's heart. I have no more insight into its inclination than you do."

Mr. Simmons pondered his words, accepting the truth in them with a nod of his head. "And what of her family? Would they be inclined towards the match?"

Again, Thomas was forced into frankness. "Her mother would be overjoyed. As to the response of her father, I should think that will depend greatly on the response of his daughter. I do not think he will refuse you, should Mar-" He cut himself off and cleared his throat, horrified that he had almost called her by her personal name in front of the other man. "Should Miss Bennet accept." He paused. "At least that is what I am given to believe, based on his other daughters' engagements."

Mr. Simmons turned on his heel and crossed to the desk to shake Thomas' hand briskly. "I am glad to hear that," he said with obvious relief. "Thank you very much, Bowen. I am much obliged for your time."

He bowed and was out the door before Thomas had even realized he was going. Thomas leaned back in his chair and let out a whoosh of breath, grateful that the uncomfortable interview was over. Then he tensed in his seat and ran a hand through his already rumpled hair. His interview with Mr. Simmons might be over, but he could not truly be at ease until Mary had refused the man—*if* she refused him. And he had no way of knowing when that was going to happen.

He could be comforted with the knowledge that she was to remain at Kaverstow for the rest of the day and would return early the following morning. Any interview on Mr. Simmons part was unlikely to occur until her next day off, but he could not be sure the man would wait that long.

He bounded out of his chair and started pacing the same line Mr. Simmons had trod. Most importantly, how was he going to keep all that had transpired from Mary? He already felt guilty, having foreknowledge of what was to occur and yet being unable to share it with her.

It was going to be a very difficult week.

*****

Thomas managed to keep to himself until Mary departed later that evening. His emotions were too turbulent to be in polite company, and he did not trust himself to keep Mr. Simmons' confidence while he was around her.

As soon as she left, though, the need for the comfort of his familial bosom became too strong, and he descended to the gardens, where he knew he would find John playing with his children.

He sat down beside his brother-in-law on a bench, while the children romped on the grass. John bounced Helene on his knee and greeted Thomas with a smile. "I thought you had disappeared. Where have you been all day? Unless I miss my guess, I would hazard to say Miss Bennet was very disappointed by your absence."

Thomas sighed deeply. "I had a visitor this morning. Mr. Simmons. He came to be reassured, I think, as to the likelihood of Miss Bennet accepting his hand in marriage."

John let out a low whistle. "I cannot say I saw that coming."

Thomas nodded fervently. "It was quite possibly the most difficult conversation of my existence."

"What did you tell him?"

"What could I tell him? The man has just as much a right as I do to ask for her hand. Perhaps even more so, with his nine thousand a year. It is not like I have a prior understanding with her or a secret engagement."

"That talk smacks soundly of despair," John cautioned him. "Best not to give up quite yet, although, I thought told you to talk to her! Must you always ignore my excellent advice?"

"I cannot do it now. It would be wrong of me to interfere, knowing he is going to make his intentions known next week."

"How do you know it is going to be next week? Did he tell you when he was going to do the deed?"

"No, but I assumed he would be unable to visit her until next week, on her day off. She will be here every day until then."

"Ah, but you have forgotten about her Mamma. What if Mr. Simmons should be invited to dinner one night?"

Thomas scoffed. "Mary would inform me, should such an event take place."

"I am sure she would," John agreed, "So long as she is aware of it."

Thomas groaned. "It would be just like Mrs. Bennet to plan a dinner party and not inform Mary."

John nodded. "You must concede it to be a likely scenario."

"Unfortunately," Thomas grumbled. "The only time she is safe from his wiles will be while she is here, in my household."

"And even then, should he show up and ask for an audience, you will not be able to prevent him from being granted one."

Thomas looked at his brother-in-law wryly. "You are of no comfort to me, John. Must you remind me of every little thing that could go wrong?"

John grinned crookedly. "If you had taken my advice, you would not be in this predicament."

*****

As involved in their conversation as they were, neither adult noticed that the children had stopped their play and were listening intently to the discussion.

"Does that mean Miss Bennet is going to leave us?" Sophia whispered, wide-eyed.

"If she gets married she has to leave us," John said. "Her new husband wouldn't let her be our governess. It's just not done."

"But I don't want Miss Bennet to leave!" Sophia sniffled. "Who would kiss my knee when I fall?"

"Hush, now," Emilia said comfortingly. "We do not know for sure that Miss Bennet would even say yes. But just in case, I think we need to take action. We can make her stay if we play our cards right."

John was intrigued by the gleam he recognized in his sister's eye. "Just what are you suggesting, Emilia?"

She rubbed her hands together maniacally, obviously pleased with herself. "What is the one way we can keep Miss Bennet with us forever?"

Sophia frowned. "I don't think Uncle Thomas would like it if we kidnapped her and tied her up in the cellar."

"No, silly!" Emilia eyed her sister with disgust. "If Uncle Thomas married her!"

John nodded approvingly. "Then she wouldn't be just the governess, she would be our aunt. And she would always be there to take care of us."

Emilia grinned. "Precisely."

Sophia frowned. "But what if Uncle Thomas and Miss Bennet don't want to get married?"

Emilia and John shared a look, and shook their heads at Sophia's naivety.

"Trust me," John said. "They want to get married. They just don't know it yet."

Emilia nodded emphatically. "Definitely."

"But how are we going to get Uncle Thomas to propose?" Sophia asked. "He said he only had one week until that other man asked her to marry him. That is not very long."

"I will tell you what we do…" Emilia gathered her siblings in closer and laid out her plan. By the end of her explanation, they were all nodding enthusiastically.

"That just might work," John said approvingly. "Now we just have to set the wheels in motion."

Emilia smirked. "We start tomorrow."

*****

They had all underestimated Mr. Simmons' impatience and Mrs. Bennet's cunning.

Mary arrived home down-hearted and confused by Thomas' absence that day, only to find Longbourn a whirlwind of activity.

"What is going on?" she asked Hill, with some degree of shock as she removed her bonnet and gloves. "Are we to have another guest?"

"No, miss. Your mother has invited Mr. Simmons to dine this evening."

Mary sighed. Just when she thought her day could not get any worse, her mother's machinations managed to do the trick. "I see."

The door to the drawing room was open and Mrs. Bennet's voice could be heard calling loudly from within, "Hill! Hill! Come in here at once! I have something I need to discuss with you!"

Mary shared a long-suffering look with Hill before the other woman slipped away to see to Mrs. Bennet. Mary hoped that would mean her mother was too busy to notice her arrival home. She tried to sneak past the open door, only to be caught in the act.

"Oh, there you are Mary! Are you just come home? Come in! Come in! I must speak with you!" Mrs. Bennet waved her in, beaming with pleasure, and then proceeded to continue her conversation with Hill.

Mary waited with ill-concealed impatience for her mother to finish, thinking of all the things she could be doing instead of waiting for her mother to get around to speaking with her.

At length, Mrs. Bennet sent Hill on her way, with an extensive list of tasks to accomplish and demands to be carried out before their guests should arrive. She turned to Mary and patted the seat beside her. "Come sit beside me, dear." She brushed the hair back from Mary's face tenderly. "Oh my dear, sweet Mary! You are to be wed at last. I cannot fathom how I have done so well by all of you. Five daughters married! It is more than I dared to hope!"

Mary's heart pounded in her breast. Could this be the reason for Thomas' absence? Dare she hope that he had been to see her father to request her hand?

"What are you speaking of Mamma?" she asked cautiously, the smallest flicker of hope burning in her heart.

"Why, Mr. Simmons, of course!" Mrs. Bennet patted Mary's cheek. "He is coming to dinner this evening and I do believe he means to propose!" She squealed, sounding much younger than her years. "Five daughters married!"

"Mr. Simmons?!" Mary stammered, mouth agape.

"Yes, dear," Mrs. Bennet said long-sufferingly. "Please do try not to appear quite so simple-minded tonight. We do not want him to change his mind and ask some other young lady, like what happened when Lizzie refused Mr. Collins, the insolent girl. But no matter, she is married, and to Mr. Darcy at that, so it all worked out in the end. But I just know Lady Lucas would be most pleased to see him settled with Maria and she is such a shameless, conniving woman. We must put our best foot forward, Mary, for you may never receive another offer!"

Mary felt her ire rising. "And what of my mind, Mamma? Have I no say in the matter?"

Mrs. Bennet was oblivious to the dangerous edge in Mary's voice. "Why of course you do, dear! You must say yes!"

Mary took a deep breath and tried to tamp down her anger. Her mother could very well be wrong about Mr. Simmons' intentions. She had certainly misread such situations in the past. It was quite possible that she was overreacting. Mary stood and said tightly, "I must get ready now, Mamma. Pray excuse me."

"Why, of course, of course!" Mrs. Bennet clucked. "You must look your best for Mr. Simmons!" She shooed Mary upstairs. "Go! Go!"

Mary went gratefully, glad to escape her mother's clutches.

She was tired after a long day with the children and in no mood to entertain, especially given her mother's revelations, but her conscience would not allow her to plead a nonexistent headache and retire for the night. She prepared herself with a sigh to go through with the ordeal. If she could but make it through the night, tomorrow would bring a new day, and hopefully, with it, Thomas.

Hill had been commanded by Mrs. Bennet to pay particular attention to Mary's toilette that evening, so before much time had passed, that lady was knocking on her door, a freshly pressed gown in her hands. "Mrs. Bennet has requested that you wear this gown tonight, Miss."

Mary was in no mood to argue. "Very well, Hill." Hill helped her into the gown and turned her to face the looking-glass. Mary blushed at the sight of her reflection, suddenly wishing she had at least inspected the gown before agreeing to wear it. She remembered it vaguely as one of Lydia's castoffs that had been remade to fit her. It had hung in the wardrobe, unworn until now, for Mrs. Bennet had had a large influence in its remaking, and the gown was far too low-cut and gaudy for Mary's tastes.

But there was no time to change now if Hill was to style her hair, and so Mary resigned herself to a night of discomfort, grateful that Thomas, at least, would not see her so vulgarly attired.

At least she had the presence of mind to insist that Hill arrange her hair in a simple yet flattering style and ignore the rouge her mother had sent along. She had no need of such cosmetics when her acute embarrassment at even the suggestion of using them was enough to color her cheeks pink.

When Hill left her, her toilette complete, Mary took a few minutes to compose herself before joining her family in the drawing room to wait for their guest to arrive. She made a face at her reflection in the mirror, disgusted by the low neckline and her easy compliance with her mother's wishes.

Although she sincerely hoped her mother was wrong about Mr. Simmons' intentions, she had a sinking feeling they were correct. She needed to prepare herself, so if the topic did come up, she was ready to face it.

She had no intention of accepting any proposal from him, no matter how disappointed her mother might be, nor how hysterical she might become. She was not going to be manipulated into marrying a man she did not love, regardless of how poor her chances at matrimony might otherwise be considered.

Mr. Simmons was a nice man, with many qualities and possessions that would make him a fine catch for another woman. But he was not Thomas.

No man could replace Thomas, regardless of his social status or wealth. She would not be happy with any other man. Even if Thomas never returned her feelings, if she was only an employee to him for the rest of her life, she could not marry another.

She would rather die an old maid, living in a cottage with twenty-seven cats and her pianoforte, than have all the money in the world and share all her days with another man.

She could not do it. And she would not allow anyone to persuade her otherwise.

If only Lizzie were here to support her! She knew her sister would be proud to see her stand firm against their mother's machinations. Lizzie would have made sure that Pappa supported her, too, like he had so long ago when Mr. Collins had been determined to marry her.

Mary wished for the confidence Lizzie possessed, the self-assurance that regardless of the consequences she was in the right, and the stubborn refusal to give in to popular opinion.

Mary tilted her chin up and struck her best Lizzie pose. She smiled at herself in the mirror. She would arm herself with a Lizzie-like attitude, and none would be able to stop her.

Thus resolved, she descended the stairs to join her family.

*****

Dinner proceeded with little fanfare. Mr. Simmons was all that was agreeable. He arrived precisely on time, complimented Mrs. Bennet on the meal, and showered Mary with every attention. He even managed to draw Mr. Bennet into the conversation around the dinner table without inciting him to sarcasm.

But he showed absolutely no inclination to propose. By the time the meal concluded, Mary was reasonably reassured that her fears had been for naught. Her mother must have mistaken his intentions.

The ladies withdrew to the drawing room at the end of the meal, leaving the men to their port. Mary breathed a sigh of relief upon gaining the room and immediately adjourned to the pianoforte in the corner, her pleasure at discovering that her worry had been unnecessary finding its expression in music.

Mrs. Bennet was undeterred by the fact that her scheme had yet to come to fruition. She was still firmly convinced that Mr. Simmons meant to propose and that he meant to do it that night.

She fluttered about the drawing room, adjusting this and rotating that so as to show off the room to its best advantage. "Come, Lydia, assist me! Everything must be just so for Mr. Simmons when he returns to propose to your sister."

Lydia rolled her eyes. "Surely you jest, Mamma. Mr. Simmons cannot have any interest in proposing to Mary, much less doing so tonight."

"You must know, my dear, that I never jest when it comes to matters of the heart," Mrs. Bennet scolded.

Mary ignored the bickering and fidgeting going on around her, instead throwing her energy into a joyful rendition of one of her favorite pieces. It was a complicated piece, requiring all of her concentration, and she was glad to lose herself in it and shut out the commotion of her mother and sister.

She realized too late that she had also drowned out the sound of her father and Mr. Simmons rejoining them in the drawing room and her family leaving her to a private audience with Mr. Simmons.

As her fingers lingered on the last rousing notes, she became aware of someone clapping.

"Brava, Miss Bennet! Brava!" Mr. Simmons said as he came forward to join her at the pianoforte.

A quick glance around the room afforded Mary the realization that they were quite alone. With a sinking heart, she tried to summon a weak smile. "I thank you, Mr. Simmons."

"That was quite a stirring performance. I do not think I have ever seen you play with such vigor and power. I am much impressed."

Mary was not sure how to respond to such unusual praise, and so remained silent.

Mr. Simmons took a deep breath to steady his nerves, and then plunged forward, sinking to one knee before her. "You must know, Miss Bennet, how deeply I admire you. I have never met another with such an exquisite mix of high morals and accomplishments. Our dispositions are so similar and our opinions of such likeness that I cannot help but feel that we would be well-suited to one another. Will you do me the honor of accepting my hand in marriage?"

Mary regarded his sincere visage and carefully worded her reply, feeling some sympathy for the man. "It is true, Mr. Simmons, that we share many of the same opinions and inclinations. But I feel it is necessary to inform you that I could not make you the sort of wife that I am convinced you deserve. I have found you to be a very kind and respectable man. You deserve a wife who can give you her whole heart unreservedly, and that is something I cannot do."

Mr. Simmons regarded her solemnly, searching her face for several moments before he responded, "You love another, then?"

There was a short pause and then Mary nodded shortly. "I do."

Mr. Simmons swallowed hard. "Well, then." He rose and turned toward the door.

"I hope you know I have no ill-will toward you, Mr. Simmons," Mary hurried to say. "I wish you the very best in your future endeavors."

Mr. Simmons turned back to grace her with a sad smile. "Never fear, Miss Bennet. I could never think such a thing of you." He bowed and was gone a moment later, pushing past her family to leave, as they were crowded round the door he pulled open unexpectedly.

Seeing three open-mouthed faces turn toward her simultaneously, Mary found she could not bear to face the questions that would undoubtedly follow her refusal. She stood and pushed passed them before they could recover. "Excuse me, but I need some time to myself." She hurried upstairs, almost tripping on the steps in her haste, and barred her bedroom door against the deluge that was already following her.

"Mary! Mary!" Her mother's sharp voice came from the other side of the door. There was a sharp rapping on the door. "Come out at once, young lady! Explain yourself!"

Mary sank to the floor, her back against the door, and cradled her head in her hands.

Mrs. Bennet did not give up the point easily. She talked to Mary through the door again and again, coaxing and threatening her by turns. But, alas! Mary was determined, and at length her continued silence was enough to dissuade Mrs. Bennet from further entreaty. She descended into petulance and went off to solicit Lydia's sympathy with repeated protestations as to the unfairness of it all and the stress upon her poor nerves. Lydia was only too happy to listen to her complaints and to add her own to the mix, and thus Mrs. Bennet had to be consoled with the loss of a prospective son-in-law.

Mary was relieved to have the matter finished. She felt some discomfort at the hurt Mr. Simmons must feel from her rejection, but could have no real remorse. It had been done in the least offensive manner possible and there could have been no happy conclusion to the matter for all parties involved.

She was satisfied with her response and could not help but hope that that which had been so distasteful to her was followed soon thereafter by a much more welcome offer.

CHAPTER FIFTEEN

When darkness had descended upon Kaverstow, at an hour far later than when they should have been abed, John, Emilia, and Sophia put their plan into action. With stealthy steps, they stole into the servant's quarters. Their plan centered on a key, and there was only one time that key was not firmly attached to the housekeeper's waist- while she slept.

They would have no other opportunity to retrieve it, and knowing this leant urgency to their mission. Silently, they passed the closed doors they had scoped out as being the maids' rooms while the servants had been busy at their work that afternoon. They paused outside the housekeeper's door to briefly review the plan, and then Emilia cracked open the door and tiptoed inside while John and Sophia guarded the entrance.

An anxiety-ridden ten minutes later, she emerged victorious, holding up one large key for their inspection. They were hard put to contain their excitement as they scurried back toward the family wing and their own rooms, but they managed to contain themselves until they had reached the hall outside the nursery.

"We did it!" Sophia squealed.

"Shhh!" Emilia scolded her. "We might have gotten the key, but if we get caught now, it is all over."

John whispered, "Yeah. We're not in the clear until Uncle Thomas and Miss Bennet are engaged. Then we'll know we actually managed to carry it off. We cannot mess this up."

They were all in agreement on this point at least, and with that firmly in mind, they scattered to their beds, ostensibly to get a good night's rest before the exciting day to come. In reality, none of them slept much, as the expectation of what was to come held far too much anticipation to be conducive to a restful night's sleep.

They were awake far before the nursemaid came in to rouse them, and were anxiously watching for Mary's arrival from the window far earlier than she could reasonably be expected.

"You do think she will come today, right?" asked Sophia.

"Of course," scoffed John. "She has not missed a day. There is no way she would start today."

Sophia said, "I hope Uncle Thomas does not get mad at us."

"He will not be mad," Emilia said. "If anything, he will be really, really happy."

"I wish I could be so sure."

"You will be, once this is over."

They were surprised by the sight of Mary, coming up the lane.

"Miss Bennet is really early," said Sophia.

Emilia worried her bottom lip. "I hope everything is alright. I don't want anything to interfere with our plan. We had better proceed cautiously."

John agreed. "It would be better to put it off for a day if we have to; rather than go ahead and have it all backfire on us. We need a code word in case we have to call it off."

Emilia frowned. "And one to use as the go ahead."

Sophia smiled. "I know! Let's use pudding and porridge! Pudding for the go ahead and porridge to back off."

John rolled his eyes as his sister's sweet tooth made another appearance, but agreed. They were easy words that could be worked into a conversation without too much difficulty.

"Are we ready?" asked Emilia.

They nodded solemnly.

"Then everyone to your stations!"

John headed out the door to join his uncle in the study, taking Duke with him, and gave the girls a jaunty wave as he went. The girls settled themselves around their little table to wait for Miss Bennet to come up.

Sophia fidgeted in her chair nervously.

"Hold still!" Emilia reprimanded her crossly. "If you don't settle down and act normal she will know something is up!"

"But I can't help it," complained Sophia. "I am just so excited!"

Mary came in at that moment and overheard Sophia's statement. "What are you so excited about, Sophia?"

Sophia shared a wide-eyed look with her sister. She bit down hard on her bottom lip. "Nothing, Miss Bennet."

"Are you sure about that?" said Mary with amusement. "It sounded like something special to me."

Emilia hurried to come to her sister's rescue, as it appeared Sophia was about to suffer an apoplexy. "We're just excited because… er…" She cast her mind about for a suitable answer. "Because Uncle Thomas said we could have pudding for dessert." She forced a smile to her lips. "You know how much Sophia loves her sweets."

"Indeed." Mary fought to control the smile that threatened to turn up the corners of her mouth. "And I also happen to know that your cook makes a very good pudding." She crossed to a cupboard and pulled out their samplers. "Are we ready to get started?"

"Pudding?" hissed Sophia while Mary's back was to them. "Does that mean we're on?"

"I don't know," hissed back Emilia. "It was all I could think of to say. But I guess we are unless one of us says porridge."

Mary turned back to bring them their samplers and they both quieted, turning angelic countenances and wide smiles toward her. She eyed them warily before handing them their samplers. She knew that look, and it meant trouble was a-brewing.

*****

John flung open his uncle's study door with a bang.

Thomas looked up with a scowl. "John, please take a care with that door. I have already had to repair enough furniture since you and your sisters have been here without adding the doors to the account."

John eyed his uncle, wondering what had gotten his tail in such a knot, before announcing, "Miss Bennet wanted to see you in the nursery."

Thomas started. "Miss Bennet is here already?"

"Yep. She was extra early this morning."

Thomas frowned. "I wonder why. Did she happen to mention if anything was amiss?"

John shrugged. "She didn't say anything to me about it."

"Of course not," Thomas murmured. "Why would she?" He rose. "I suppose I should see what she wanted then."

John trailed his uncle out the door, pleased as punch that his part had gone without a hitch. That had been much easier to accomplish than he had expected. His uncle had no idea anything out of the ordinary was going on.

*****

Mary looked up in surprise when a knock sounded unexpectedly at the door. She rose to answer it. "Mr. Bowen, what a pleasant surprise!" She opened the door so Thomas could step inside. "To what do we owe your visit?"

His brow furrowed. "I beg your pardon?"

"I asked, to what do we owe your visit? It is not often you come up to the nursery unannounced."

Thomas was thoroughly confused. "But, I th-"

"Pudding!" shouted John before all their work could be undone, and all three of the children sprang into action, converging on Thomas and Mary and pushing them into the closet. Sophia and John held the door shut while Emilia produced her pilfered key and locked the door with a flourish.

It all happened so quickly and unexpectedly that neither Thomas nor Mary had time to protest before they found themselves facing each other, alone in the dark closet.

Thomas could not see Mary's face, but he could hear her labored breathing. He had a sudden flashback to her panic attack in the cave and prayed that there were not any spiders hiding in the cramped confines of the closet. He might not make it out with all his bits intact if there were.

He pounded on the closet door. "Let us out this instant! You three are in big trouble! BIG TROUBLE!"

There was silence from the other side of the door, and then as his eyes adjusted to the darkness, Thomas could make out a thin piece of paper being slid under the door.

He picked it up and squinted at the childish scrawl, but it was too dark to make out the words. "There is no way I can read this in the dark."

A single match slid under the door. He picked it up. "I would have preferred you just open the door."

"I would be more concerned that the children have access to matches," Mary quipped, in an attempt at levity.

Thomas just grimaced and lit the match on his boot, the flickering light illuminating his face as he read the children's demands. Mary saw the faint traces of a smile curling his lips upwards before the match burnt out and they descended back into darkness.

"Well?" she demanded. "What did it say?"

She could hear the smile in his voice as he responded, "Their demands were not unreasonable. Just a little premature, I think."

Another piece of paper was shoved under the door, along with a match. This time, Thomas frowned as he read the note. "Apparently, they feel it is not premature but past time. And they are prepared to wait us out. I suggest you make yourself comfortable, Miss Bennet. I have a feeling this standoff is not going to end anytime soon."

"You are not going to give in to their demands?"

"Of course not! Any adult knows that they cannot allow the children to usurp their authority by giving in to their every demand."

"I do believe this to be an extraordinary circumstance, Thomas. Surely, giving in just this once would do no harm."

"What would I be teaching them if I gave in? That anytime they want something they cannot have all they have to do is lock us in a closet? Surely not!"

"Are their demands really that unreasonable?"

Thomas sighed. "No. In fact, I would gladly comply if I could. But there are extenuating circumstances that make it impossible for me to follow through with what they want."

"Oh." Mary was silent for a few moments as she contemplated his words. "Well, surely one of the servants will come along at some point and discover they have locked us in here. The housekeeper has a key to every lock, does she not? She will be able to release us."

"Yes. I believe that to be our best course of action. We shall have to be content to bide our time until then."

"Well, in that case, I do believe I shall make myself more comfortable."

Thomas heard rustling as she seated herself on the floor with her back against the side wall. He smiled and followed suit so that they were facing each other in the crowded space. He stretched out his legs to one side and she smoothed her skirts over her own. Noises coming from the other side of the door suggested that the children were also making themselves comfortable on the opposite side of the room.

"So," Mary said quietly. "Has there been any decision as to where the children are going?"

Thomas grinned. "Actually, yes. My brother-in-law spoke to me about that very subject just this morning."

Mary was pleased to finally have closure on the topic. "Really? I am so glad! Please, do tell me."

"They are staying. John said he could not imagine uprooting them now that they have come to view Kaverstow as their home."

Mary clapped her hands gleefully. "Oh! I am so happy! I could not stand the thought of them being taken away from us. It was just too much!"

Thomas nodded. "I know. I am glad they did not even know it was a possibility. Could you imagine the uproar we would have had on our hands then? I am not sure even their father could have controlled them! But it is nice to have it all settled."

"I agree. I do not like having such uncertainties. I was fretting about it constantly. It is a relief to no longer have it hanging over me."

Their eyes were growing accustomed to the darkness and Thomas could make out the gentle curve of her cheek and the happy tilt of her mouth. His heart pounded and he longed to do what the note had suggested- ask Mary to marry him. But he could not, not yet. Not when he knew another man had laid claim to that honor first. He could not interfere, not until he knew she had made her choice and was free to answer him.

He took a deep breath and tried to distract himself from her nearness. "What of you? Did anything interesting happen yesterday? I am sorry I was not around. I had an unexpected visitor."

She turned her face away, even though she knew he would not be able to read her expression in the darkness. She knew he was only asking about her day with the children. There was no way he could know about Mr. Simmons and his proposal. Still, it was difficult to think of anything else. "I, too, had an unexpected visitor."

"Here? At Kaverstow?" His voice conveyed mild alarm. Mr. Simmons could not have sought her out under his own roof without Thomas' knowledge, could he? Surely Bertram would have informed him if such was the case.

"No. At Longbourn. My mother had arranged for a dinner party last night without my knowledge. It was… eventful."

Thomas was relieved. "Eventful? In what way?"

"My mother had invited Mr. Simmons to dine with us."

Thomas' heart clenched in his chest. He swallowed back the panic that threatened to overwhelm him and forced words passed his lips. He had to know. "She did? Did…did he ask you something?"

Mary really did not want to discuss such a sensitive subject with him without some assurance that he felt the same way about her that she did about him. But the words tumbled out of her mouth of their own volition. "He asked me for my hand in marriage."

"And? What was your answer? Did you accept him?" Thomas' voice was hard, demanding, his fear making him irrational.

"I did not."

The fight drained out of Thomas in an instant, replaced by pure, effervescent joy. He leaned forward to cradle her face in his hands. "My dear, sweet Mary! That was quite possibly the most foolish decision you have ever made, but I am so glad you did not accept him!"

Her breath hitched. Could it be? Was it possible? She had to know. "Why, Thomas? Why are you glad?"

He laughed, his worries and misgivings gone in a tide of unadulterated relief. "Because, you silly girl, I love you! And you would make me the happiest man alive if you would marry *me*!"

She smiled tremulously. "I love you, too, Thomas. And it would make me ever so happy to marry you."

He pulled her to him, crushing her against his chest and murmuring in her hair, "You cannot know how I have longed to hear those words from you."

Mary smiled and stroked his chest. "Yes I can."

Thomas laughed. He pulled away from her slightly to look down at her. "I suppose you can." He stroked her cheek and dropped his head until his lips were a whisper away from hers and murmured, "And I suppose you know exactly how I'm feeling right now."

Her nod was almost imperceptible. "Mm Hmm."

He held her in suspense for a moment longer, then dipped his head and brushed her lips with his own.

The kiss was soft, gentle, tender. It held a promise for the future to come. *Their* future. It erased every fear and trepidation that they had felt along the journey to that moment and replaced them with hope and security.

In that moment, it did not matter that Thomas did not have nine thousand pounds a year, or that they were being held hostage by the three children they would be raising together.

They were *right*. They fit. No one else could fill the space in their heart where the other belonged.

CHAPTER SIXTEEN

Quite some time passed after that, during which the young couple was far too wrapped up in grinning foolishly at one another and whispering sweet nothings and endearments to notice the passage of time.

Nor did they heed the distinct *click* of the lock being opened.

It was not until the door was pulled open and light flooded in that they looked up. Three small faces and one adult one peered down at them.

John frowned at the sight of them wrapped in each other's arms and wrinkled his nose distastefully. "Eww! They were kissing."

Emilia grinned. "Well, I think it is romantic!"

"Me, too!" agreed Sophia.

Their father just dropped a knowing wink at the blushing couple in the closet. "I think you two can come out now, if I do not miss my guess."

They scrambled to their feet, Thomas solicitously helping Mary off the floor. He cleared his throat while Mary tried unsuccessfully to hide the flush that heated her cheeks. "I think Miss Bennet and I need to go speak with her father, so lessons are canceled for the day." He shared a look with his grinning brother-in-law. "I trust your father can handle you three?"

Their father chuckled and nodded. "Leave them to me." He shooed them out the door. "You have bigger problems to deal with."

When the door had closed behind them, John looked down at his mischievous brood and shook his head with a grin. "While I cannot fault your motives, your method could have used a little more thought."

"It worked, didn't it?" his son said belligerently. "They are going to get married."

"Yes," John agreed. "I am just as happy as you are about that. But you stole a key from the housekeeper and locked your uncle and your governess in a closet. You are not going to get off without any repercussions for your actions."

Sophia cocked her head. "What does repercussions mean?"

Her brother sighed. "It means we're in trouble, that's what."

Sophia eyed her father warily. "Uh oh."

*****

Mr. Bennet, fortunately, had enough foresight to believe that his daughter's refusal the night before might lead to another, happier, knock on his study door that evening. He was not surprised, then, when Hill admitted the young couple into his study.

His blessing was asked for, and given, with little fanfare or emotion. And yet, upon their departure to inform Mrs. Bennet, and amid the resulting shrieking, he could not help but reflect with a sad smile upon the very great privilege of having five daughters married.

*****

Mrs. Bennet's nerves were thrown into conniptions when Mary informed her that she had no interest in having a new dress made for her wedding and that she was unwilling to go to London to shop for her trousseau.

Mary's wish was simple- to become Thomas' wife as quickly and as easily as possible. No dress could hold much appeal when compared to that prospect.

And so they were married as soon as a license could be obtained and the banns read.

It was a simple, elegant ceremony, and the wedding breakfast that followed was a joyous occasion. All five Bennet sisters had managed to make it for the occasion, husbands and children in tow, with the notable exception of Mr. Wickham.

John, Emilia, Sophia, and Helene were overjoyed by the sudden extension of their family and the cousins they thus gained. Thomas, on the other hand, was somewhat overwhelmed by the extended family, having never had much interaction with the illustrious Mr. Darcy, the jovial Mr. Bingley, or the renowned Lord Rockingham, Nathaniel Watson, and did not hesitate to tell his new wife so, when they retired that night.

"I have never been in a room with such prestigious and well-known men in my life. I just wanted to cower in the corner. I hardly dared to speak a word in their presence."

Mary laughed. "They can be quite intimidating, can they not? And Mr. Darcy always looks so cross when he is forced into social situations. But they are all very nice, once you get to know them, and they love my sisters very much."

"Yes, I could see that. The only time Mr. Darcy smiled at all was when he was looking at your sister Elizabeth, while Lord Rockingham and Bingley could not seem to *stop* smiling."

Mary grinned wickedly. "You were not so very poised, either. If I recall correctly, I never saw you without a smile on your face."

"That is because I never had to leave my beautiful bride's side. And as long as can I remain there, you will never see me without a smile on my face."

Mary's smile softened and she reached up to caress his cheek. "I hope we are never parted, then."

Their gaze caught and held, and then Thomas' gaze sank to rest firmly on her mouth. He dropped his head and closed the distance between them to capture her lips with his own, ready to explore what their future held.

And just in case there was any doubt in your mind, dear reader, from that moment on they lived happily ever after.

EPILOGUE

Ten years later…

Mary was relieved when their carriage crested the hill and Cheventhorpe appeared in the distance. Kitty did not live as far away from Hertfordshire as Jane or Elizabeth did, but it was still a difficult journey to make with five small children.

The baby, Charity, had fallen asleep to the rocking of the carriage an hour ago, and Mary sent up a brief prayer, thanking God for small favors. The poor little thing was teething and the pain had kept her, and by extension, Mary, up all night.

Thomas had their three-year-old, Penelope, engaged in pointing out the scenery and animals as they passed. She was chattering away, her lisp making some of her words indecipherable to all but those most familiar with her. Thomas, of course, had no such problems understanding his daughter, and was more than happy to listen to all she had to say, as there had been a time, not yet forgotten, when they had worried she might never speak at all.

Five-year-old Prudence straightened up in her seat beside Mary at the sight of Cheventhorpe. "Are we almost there, Mamma?"

"Yes, very nearly," said Mary.

It was not the first time they had been to Cheventhorpe, nor was it likely to be their last, but it was unique in that the entire extended family was to come, with the usual exception of George Wickham.

Mary was looking forward to the opportunity to be with her sisters again. Even with the additions to their families, and the distractions these necessitated, it had been far too long since they had been all together. Letters were no substitute for seeing them in person.

The carriage ground to a halt in front of Cheventhorpe's grand entrance, and Mary shook her head wryly at the thought of her little sister as the mistress of such grandeur. She never would have believed it of the boy-crazy, wild young woman she had been, but Kitty had certainly come a long way since then.

Lady Rockingham, as she was known now, was respected and well-liked in this neighborhood, despite her propensity to race across the fields on horseback and join her children in sliding down the banisters of their great home.

Thomas stepped out of the carriage and swung Penelope down, eliciting a giggle. He would have happily done the same with Prudence, but she had informed them quite seriously just that week that she was far too old for such shenanigans. Instead, she primly took the hand he offered her and stepped down.

Thomas reached back inside to take the baby, which Mary handed off gingerly. Charity stirred as her father settled her against his shoulder, but did not wake. Mary breathed a sigh of relief and allowed her husband to help her out of the carriage.

The second carriage pulled to a halt behind the first, and John came riding up beside it, dismounting quickly so he could open the carriage door and help out his sisters and cousins. At twenty, he cut quite the dashing figure. He was still a little reckless and wild and stubborn to a fault, but Mary had hope that a few more years would find him settled down.

Emilia was the first to be handed down from the second carriage. She stepped back out of the way to brush the travel dust from her skirts. She was a beautiful young woman of eighteen now. She was poised and elegant, but her mischievous streak still showed itself regularly. Thankfully, her machinations were now generally aimed toward the young gentlemen of her acquaintance, instead of Thomas and Mary. It was perhaps not the most proper trait for a young lady to display, but as it kept the more amorous of suitors at bay, Mary let her behavior slide.

Sophia was next out of the carriage, followed quickly by Helene, Hannah, and Ruth.

Mary turned from supervising the unloading when she heard a voice calling her name. She grinned at the sight of her sister, flying down the stairs with open arms to greet her. She was glad she had handed the baby off to Thomas as Kitty crushed her in her embrace.

"I am so pleased you have come!" Kitty squealed. "Nathaniel and I have been so looking forward to your visit, and the children are dying to play with their cousins!" Kitty pulled back long enough to send an appraising eye over her. "But what am I saying? You must be exhausted after your trip. Come, let me show you to your rooms so you can rest. We can catch up over dinner."

Kitty prodded her in the direction of the stairs, where their husbands were waiting, but Mary could not help but send a glance over her shoulder at her children.

"Do not worry," Kitty told her. "I have instructed the housekeeper to show the older ones to their rooms and your nurse and the little ones to the nursery, as well. They will be fine."

Mary noticed that Thomas had already handed Charity off to the nurse and the housekeeper seemed to have everything well in hand, despite the size of their party. She allowed her sister to steer her inside.

"Has anyone else arrived yet?" Mary asked as they walked. Cheventhorpe was a massive building and the guest rooms were located some distance from the main entrance.

"Lydia is here, with Antonia," Kitty said. "They have been here for a week already, for as you know she is never one to pass up an opportunity for a visit. I believe she is lying down at the moment, or surely she would have been out to greet you as well. The Bingleys and the Darcys are to arrive this afternoon, and both sets of Crosbys tomorrow. Richard and Anne arrive the day after that."

"I hope you have a large nursery," Mary commented. "How many children are there between all of us? Twenty-five?"

"Twenty-eight," Kitty said with humor. "And twenty-one of those are under the age of ten."

"Three of mine no longer really count as children anymore."

"You are fortunate to have their help with your little ones."

"Trust me; I do not take that for granted!" Mary said with a light laugh. "But I am not sure that their help now has made up for the trouble they caused us when they were younger."

Kitty laughed. "They were certainly lively children."

"They were too smart for their own good," Mary amended. "They still are. But I love them anyway. Who knows how things might have turned out without their interference?"

"I ask myself that same question sometimes," Kitty said.

"How are your children?" Mary asked. "Are they with their nurse?"

Kate nodded. "I did not want them to be overly excited by the arrivals today, so I have kept them upstairs with the nurse. The twins still need their naps and I know there is no way that would have happened if they were downstairs with us."

They stopped in front of a set of doors.

"Here are your rooms," she said. "I trust that everything is in order, but if you have need of anything, just ring for one of the servants." She gave Mary one last squeeze. "It has been far too long since we have all been together. You cannot know how I have been looking forward to this!"

Mary smiled at her enthusiasm. "I think I can imagine." She was rewarded with another hug from her sister before she was allowed to follow Thomas into their rooms.

The hustle of the subsequent arrivals did not penetrate to the guest wing, and Mary was all too happy for the brief respite after being up all night with Charity. She took the opportunity to settle in for a nap. When she awoke sometime later, it was to find Thomas ensconced in an arm chair nearby, perusing a book she could only assume he had pilfered from Cheventhorpe's library.

He looked up at the sound of her stirring. "I am glad you are up. It is almost time to dress for dinner, and I did not want to have to be the one to wake you."

She rubbed her eyes and leveraged herself into a sitting position on the side of the bed. "I see you have been orienting yourself already."

He grinned. "I have to get lost and find my way around again before everyone else is here or the fellows will make prodigious fun of me."

Mary raised an eyebrow. "I highly doubt that."

"Very well," Thomas admitted. "They may not make *prodigious* fun of me. But it would be difficult to live it down if the butler had to come rescue me *again*."

Compared to Kaverstow, Cheventhorpe was mammoth, with even Pemberly paling in comparison to it. Mary had even been lost in its halls at one point, although she was loathe to admit it. The Darcys had an easier time maneuvering through the maze of corridors than the Bowens did, but they too had trouble finding the breakfast room upon occasion.

Mary chuckled. "Perhaps." A knock at the door heralded the arrival of her ladies' maid and his valet, and they separated to dress for dinner.

A short while later, they joined the others in the drawing room before they went in to dine. Mary was pleased to see that John, Emilia, and Sophia, who were all old enough now to dine with the adults, had made it down on time.

She was proud of the ease with which they mingled among her sisters and their husbands. Even though they had spent many of their formative years tucked away in Hertfordshire, they had the presence of mind and decorum to do themselves justice in polite society.

Their parents would be proud of who they had become. Thomas still kept in touch with their father, who was even now at sea. On the rare occasions when he was home, he never failed to make the trip to Kaverstow to visit his children. That trip would become increasingly difficult in the years to come, as his children moved on and had families of their own, but for now they were all still at Kaverstow.

John was likely to remain there always. Thomas had trained him well in the management of his estate, and given the unlikelihood of them producing a male heir after five daughters, he was to take over the estate when the time came.

Kitty, Elizabeth, and Jane looked up as she and Thomas entered the room and eagerly flocked over to welcome her. Thomas abandoned her with a wink to their warm embrace, choosing instead to join their husbands in a semi-circle around the fireplace.

"Where is Lydia?" Mary asked looking around for their wayward sister.

Kitty gestured dismissively. "She asked to have a tray sent up to her room. She gave me some vague excuse about a headache."

Mary nodded, understanding perfectly. As much as they all loved their sister, and adored her daughter, they were all tired of her selfish and manipulative ways. Ever since Wickham had disappeared from her life soon after the birth of his daughter, she was forever bouncing around from one of their homes to another. She never stayed in one place long, but while she was there she took as much advantage of the situation as she could.

Mary saw her perhaps the most, for Mrs. Bennet never tired of her youngest daughter's company, and whenever Lydia could not incite one of her sisters to take her in, she could always be assured of a warm welcome at Longbourn.

Her sisters did not begrudge her the assistance she so desperately needed, especially since the arrival of Antonia, but they did resent her callous attitude toward their generosity. Time had not improved her disposition, only giving her an even more inflated view of her own self-worth.

Mrs. Bennet alone remained determined in her approval of her youngest daughter and Lydia, recognizing this, was quick to apply to her when she felt one of her sisters had slighted her. It was an uncomfortable situation, and unfortunately, one that was not likely to be resolved any time soon.

Kitty added, "I am hopeful that she will join us tomorrow. I would like Antonia to be able to spend some time in the gardens with her cousins."

There were murmurs of agreement all around, as the sweet-tempered little girl had won over all their hearts and wormed her way into her cousins' affections as well.

It was time to go in to dine, and so the party moved into the dining room, where cheerful conversation and laughter overcame any lingering ennui they might have felt at Lydia's absence.

With such an enjoyable evening behind them, Mary and Thomas could only look forward to what delights awaited them when the whole party was together in two days time. They were not as intimately acquainted with the Crosbys and the Fitzwilliams as other members of their family were, but what little they did know held promise for the days ahead.

And when, in two days, the said families had arrived, Thomas and Mary were not disappointed upon furthering their acquaintance with them. Both Crosby brothers were generally well-read and well-liked, and Colonel Fitzwilliam was all that was affable. Anne Fitzwilliam, although her health had never been particularly robust, had a surprisingly dry sense of humor and leaned towards good-natured forthrightness; all of this conspired to quickly render her a favorite among the Bennet sisters.

Georgiana, although initially reserved, soon came out from behind her mask. Even Caroline Crosby, despite her cynical and sometimes rude demeanor, had been softened somewhat by motherhood, and strove to make herself agreeable to all those present. While she was not always successful in this endeavor, the effort was appreciated by all present.

One day, a week into the visit, they were all gathered under a tent erected on the lawn, enjoying the mild weather of early summer. The smaller children romped on the lawn under the watchful eyes of their parents, while those that deemed themselves too old for such nonsense entertained themselves with a book or needlework.

A light breeze tickled Mary's neck and the delicate scent of grass and the outdoors mingled with the delightful scent of the baby on her lap. The bright sunlight was filtered by the canvas tent, shading them from the worst of the sun's heat. Birds warbled and flitted overhead, diving and soaring amidst the billowing clouds that dotted the crisp blue sky and lending their joyful song to the party.

The men were happily ensconced in one corner, discussing crop rotation methods and various other topics related to the running of their estates.

Mary was pleased to see John joining in on these conversations, expressing his opinions with confidence on those topics he was familiar with and asking insightful questions on those of which he knew little. Thomas had taught him well. Even more, he had instilled in him the self-confidence he needed to speak up in a room filled with influential men, without becoming arrogant.

Mary bounced her littlest one, Charity, on her lap, trying to coax a giggle from the girl. Emilia leaned over from her seat beside Mary to tickle the little girl under the chin when Mary's attempts proved unsuccessful.

"Come on, Charity, give me a smile," Emilia said. "You have the prettiest smile. Why do you not want to show it off for all your cousins to see?"

"She's teething," Mary told her. "I am just trying to be grateful she is not crying incessantly."

Emilia wrinkled her nose. "I remember when Penelope went through that phase. I thought we would never be able to sleep again."

Sophia groaned. "I hope Charity does not start that. I had the most dreadful headaches for months!"

"She outgrew it then, and Charity will, too," said Mary. "We just have to be patient."

"Just be glad we no longer have to share the nursery with her," Sophia chimed in. "Can you imagine what it is like now, with all those children upstairs?" She shuddered. "It must be a madhouse at meals and bedtime!"

Mary laughed. "I am sure we are all grateful for the nursemaids and their help."

"I, for one, could certainly never accomplish anything without their assistance," Kitty chimed in. "When the twins were born, Lucille was the only reason I managed to sleep at all."

There were murmurs of agreement from all the other married ladies.

"Let that be a lesson to you two for when you have families of your own," Mary advised her nieces. "Never underestimate the servants and their value. An appreciated servant is far more likely to carry out her duties diligently than one who feels you could not care less about her."

Emilia rolled her eyes good-naturedly. "You act as though we are going to run off and get married at any moment."

"Well, you have certainly had your fair share of suitors. And after some of the pranks you have pulled on them, Thomas and I half expect one of them to haul you off and cart you away to Gretna Green!" Mary shook her head teasingly. "Then we would be back to chasing after you all over again."

Emilia blushed and looked away, causing Mary to regret her teasing.

She reached out to gently touch Emilia's arm. "You will meet the right man someday, dear, and when you do, I want you to be prepared." She smiled at Sophia. "Both of you."

Emilia relented and turned her head to smile back at her aunt. Mary's teasing might strike a little too close to home for comfort, but she knew that her aunt meant her words to be taken in good fun.

"And when we say "the right man," we do not mean just any single young man with a large fortune, regardless of what our mother may tell you otherwise," Elizabeth quipped.

They all laughed, Mrs. Bennet's schemes at matchmaking being well known to all and sundry acquainted with her.

Jane cast a loving glance towards her dear Bingley. "We mean someone who will make you happy."

"And who will encourage your dreams," added Kitty.

"And who will respect you and listen to your opinions," said Elizabeth.

"Someone who will see the real you," said Georgiana.

Caroline chimed in, adding, "And who will push you to be a better person."

"Someone who is strong where you are weak, and is not afraid to stand up for you and your needs," said Anne.

"And he should be dashingly handsome!" said Lydia with a giggle, causing strained smiles and nervous laughter all around.

Mary snuggled her daughter closer and regarded her surrogate ones seriously. "Who that person is and the qualities that will make you love him will be different for each of you, but the outcome will be the same. I would rather see you remain single than enter into a loveless marriage, and I know Thomas feels the same way."

Sophia rolled her eyes. "We know, Aunt Mary. You tell us that all the time. Why do you think Emilia keeps scaring off all her suitors?"

They all laughed. With the mood sufficiently lightened by Sophia's statement, they moved on to other topics, inane conversation and pleasant banter flowing smoothly as the afternoon passed pleasantly. Mary's mind wandered and her gaze drifted to her husband, who, she noted, was watching the children playing, a wistful smile tugging at the corners of his lips.

*****

Thomas had long ago lost interest in the conversations that swirled around him. His attention was instead caught by four little girls cavorting on the lawn.

They ranged in age from nine years old to three, and while two laid claim to his own tow-headed locks, the others sported their mother's brunette tresses.

There were leaves in their hair and dirt on their pinafores. They shrieked and giggled and squealed as they played, and Thomas had no doubt that they would wreak havoc on the little sanity he had left after raising his sister's four children.

But the light in their eyes and the joy in their happy shrieks meant more to him than his own comfort and routine ever had.

He did not care that his curtains had never recovered from the brutal beating they had taken upon his nephew and nieces' arrival ten years ago. He did not care that his carpets would never be clean or that the potted plants were in constant jeopardy.

He did not even care that the door to his study never remained shut anymore.

He no longer wondered how he would live with the constant caterwauling and squealing that reverberated throughout his entire home.

Instead, he wondered how he would ever live without it.

Mary managed to catch his eye, her smile telling him she knew exactly where his thoughts were. They exchanged a tender gaze, one that encompassed all the love and laughter and dreams they had shared in the ten years since their marriage.

Neither of them could know what the future held for them, but one thing was certain. Regardless of the trials and tribulations that would come with raising nine children, their future was just as bright as their past.

Don't miss the next book by Lelia M. Silver!

An Unlikely Bride

CHAPTER ONE

Colonel Richard Fitzwilliam crumpled the missive his butler had delivered only moments before and seriously considered the merits of tossing it in the fire burning in the hearth.

He was tired of being ordered about. It was one of the many reasons why he had sold his commission, retired, and now resided at his family's townhouse in London. He eyed the roaring fire. It would give him immense satisfaction to see the flames devour the rudely worded note. He had received many commands over his years in the military, but none of them had ever come close to the imperious tone of his Aunt Catherine's summons.

He sighed and rubbed his forehead. Unfortunately, he did not have the luxury of ignoring his aunt's missive. His family expected him to wait upon her, if for nothing else than to preserve the peace.

His cousin Darcy had married only a few months before, and his aunt had not made the adjustment well. She had always expected a match between Darcy and her own daughter, Anne. To have her daughter's position stolen by a young upstart like Elizabeth Bennet had been a serious blow for the older woman.

There had been rumors Lady Catherine had taken to her bed ill for three weeks. Fitzwilliam did not put much stock in those rumors. He could no more imagine his aunt taking to her bed than he could imagine Darcy married to the quiet, sensible Anne. He thought it far more likely she had flown into a rage that even her supercilious parson, Mr. Collins, would have been hard-pressed to bring her out of.

Of course, he had not been around Rosings at the time to know the truth. In all likelihood, the only person who knew the true nature of his aunt's reaction was his cousin Anne. Considering her poor health and retiring nature, he was unlikely to get more than a generic account of what had transpired from her. Anne had always been cowed by her more aggressive mother.

It was why he had always thought she and Darcy would be completely unsuitable for one another, not that anyone cared about his opinion on the matter. On the other hand, Elizabeth Darcy had all the fire and intelligence to match Darcy tit for tat. Fitzwilliam smiled to himself. Now that was the sort of match he would not mind for himself.

However, with Darcy out of the picture, thanks to his insistence that Aunt Catherine accept his new bride, which was something she had no intention of doing, Fitzwilliam was left on his own to see to the annual review of his aunt's estates. And if the tone of her letter was any indication, she expected Fitzwilliam to attend her post-haste.

Resigning himself to the idea, Fitzwilliam smoothed out the crumpled paper and ran his fingers over the ridges he had put in the crisp parchment as he read his aunt's directives one more time.

She expected him at Rosings in one week. It would be difficult to get his affairs arranged in time to make that deadline, but not impossible.

He stood to ring for the butler. There was no time like the present to get to work.

*****

One week later, Fitzwilliam turned his horse down the lane that led to Rosings. His mount slowed as they neared the parsonage, as if he, too, was reluctant to arrive at their destination.

Fitzwilliam reached out to pat the animal's neck with one gloved hand and chuckled. "It is only for a little while," he reassured the old chap. They had been through a lot together, he and Andronicus. This was just one more battle to be fought and won, one more field to conquer.

The horse snorted, as if he did not believe him.

Fitzwilliam shook his head. "Really. We shall be here a fortnight tops, less if Darcy left the books in good order. Last year we were done in record time." He smiled a little to himself. "Although we might have Elizabeth Bennet to thank for that."

Andronicus bobbed his head in agreement and then let out a welcoming whinny that made Fitzwilliam crane his head around to see what had caught the stallion's fancy. He grinned as he caught sight of his cousin, climbing into her pony cart in front of the parsonage. The parson's wife was expecting a child soon. No doubt Anne had been sent to help Mrs. Collins with preparations for the baby.

She had not yet noticed his arrival. He took a moment to survey her as she settled into the cart and picked up the reins. She looked well. Healthier than he had seen her in years. There was color in her cheeks and a luster to her hair that had been missing before. Why, she was almost beautiful in her own sort of way.

He would never have believed it possible. Surrounded by her overbearing mother and the dark furnishings of Rosings, Anne had always seemed a little drab and rundown. He had rarely seen her in the bright light of a sunny day and he was amazed by the transformation in her.

As he watched, she lifted her face to the sun and smiled, the simple gesture transforming her features. He did not think he had ever seen someone so content and at peace as she was. At that moment, she was not just almost beautiful. She was downright breathtaking. No other woman of his acquaintance could compare to her.

Shocked, he did not even realize he had reined his mount to a standstill. Why had he never noticed this side of his cousin? Had he really been so oblivious to her? To his chagrin, he realized he had never really given her a second thought, much less a second glance.

His last visit to Rosings had been eclipsed by the obvious chemistry between Darcy and Elizabeth. Prior to that, he had always been so busy avoiding Lady Catherine and riding the estate with Darcy that he had only ever spent a few hours over dinner with his cousin.

He just might have to change that.

She lifted her hands to shake the reins over her pony's back, reminding him he was still standing in the middle of the lane, gawking at her. He closed his mouth and goaded Andronicus into motion, calling out with a cheerful grin, "Hello, Cousin!"

She turned at the sound of his voice to spy him coming up the lane toward her and rewarded him for the greeting with a heartfelt smile. "Cousin Richard! What a pleasant surprise! Mother and I were not expecting you to arrive until this evening."

He reined in his mount beside her cart. "I managed to make good time on the roads, thanks to my faithful steed here."

Andronicus shook his head prettily, making his mane fly, and preened.

Anne laughed, a lovely sound Richard could not remember ever hearing before. Then again, who could laugh in Aunt Catherine's company? She would surely reprimand them for the unseemly display. He grinned, enjoying the slightly rebellious act even more so because it was Anne that had done it.

His lovely cousin was not at all what he had expected.

Anne reached out to pet Andronicus' nose, her calm touch stilling the restless animal. "He is a fine gentleman, much like his owner."

Richard tried not to let his own chest puff up at her praise. "Thank you, Cousin. I am not sure your mother would agree with you, but the sentiment is appreciated- by both Andronicus and me."

Anne picked up the lines again. "Speaking of my mother, she has enlisted Cook's help to make all your favorite dishes tonight. I think she is determined to win you over to her side since Darcy went against her wishes." Her mouth twitched, but it was her eyes that gave away her humor with the situation.

He grimaced. "Spare me, please. I am only here to do my duty."

The smile dancing in her eyes disappeared and her spine straightened, making him instantly regret his hastily spoken words. "Of course. I would not expect otherwise. You have always been most responsible when it comes to your familial duties. Mother and I appreciate your diligence, especially since the entirety of the work will fall to you this year." She glanced at Rosings, just visible through the trees. "Mother will be expecting me. I must be going." Her gaze was disappointed as she slapped the reins over the pony's back, as if she thought she had gained an ally and then had him stolen away from her.

He sighed and watched her pull away. "Not much of a gentleman now, am I, Andronicus?"

The horse snorted his agreement, crooking Richard's mouth into a half smile. "Well, you need not have been so vehement."

The horse bobbed his head, as if to say it had been absolutely necessary. Richard had to admit, the horse was probably right.

"Do not worry, old chap. I am man enough to know when I should apologize." He kicked the horse into a trot, catching up to Anne's cart quickly.

She glanced at him from the corner of her eye but otherwise did not acknowledge him. He resisted the urge to sigh. She was not going to make this easy for him.

He did not wait for her to make eye contact. "Anne, I do apologize. I spoke without thinking and I do not wish for you to misconstrue my statement. I simply meant that I have no wish to be courted or manipulated by your mother. My feelings toward her are no reflection of my feelings toward you. Indeed, I find I barely know you, Cousin. Tell me, what news is there at Rosings?"

For an instant, he thought she was going to refuse to be reconciled, but then she relented, throwing him a small smile. Her shoulders relaxed. "There is not much news to tell. The winter was difficult, but now that spring is upon us I find myself looking forward to the change in weather and circumstances. Mrs. Collins has been a great companion to me these many months since Mrs. Jenkins left me. I think you will find her presence in the dining room to be very refreshing."

It was perhaps the longest speech Richard had ever heard his cousin utter, and he was not entirely sure how to respond. He did not wish to risk offending her again by stating his true opinion, yet he could not quite keep the skepticism out of his voice. "I have no doubt."

To his surprise, she chuckled. "You may keep your doubts, Cousin, but I take whatever small favors are granted me. Mrs. Collins is a welcome voice of reason around the table, although too often her words are discarded by the other guests. My mother is not the only one who likes to hear herself speak."

Flabbergasted by her forthright speech, Richard could not find a response. It was all he could do to close his gaping mouth.

She sent him a smile that dimpled her cheek becomingly. "You are shocked I see. It is not easy to have our closely held expectations challenged. It was Mrs. Darcy's greatest fault. She was forever challenging Mother. Yet, I cannot fault her when I have longed to do the same myself. I simply accept that should I wish to enjoy a peaceful existence in the same house as my mother, I must choose when to hold my tongue and when to let it loose. My mother is not all bad, Richard, despite what you have experienced." It was the first time she had called him simply by his given name.

Richard was silent for a moment before turning a contemplative gaze on her. "It seems nothing is as I expected it to be, Anne, least of all you. I shall look forward to having any further expectations challenged."

He tipped his hat to her and took the fork in the road that led to the front door, where he would be expected to present himself.

She steered her pony and cart around the back of the house to the stables, smiling a little to herself. Fitzwilliam was not the only one who had discovered his expectations were quite mistaken. She found herself just as eager as he was to see what other wrong assumptions she had made about her cousin.

*****

Anne entered the house through the back door. Her mother would have been appalled to find her using the servants' entrance, but Anne rather enjoyed entering through the warm kitchen, bustling with activity. It reminded her that not all at Rosings was as it appeared on the surface.

The servants had looked at her askance the first few times she had dared to do it, but now they were as accustomed to her presence as they were to the long worktable that ran the length of the room. It helped that Anne had long ago perfected the art of fading into the background.

Today, the downstairs was even more abuzz with activity than usual, thanks to the arrival of their guest. Cook and her assistants were busy preparing all of Richard's favorite foods, thanks to the cook at his parent's townhouse, who had been convinced to send round his recipes. Anne was not sure what her mother had written in her note to convince the man, but she knew her mother well enough to send a note of her own with her profuse thanks and some monetary compensation for the man's help.

She had personally overseen the preparations to Richard's room. The chamber she had chosen for his stay was different than the one he had previously used, and she hoped he would not question the change. She had moved him to one of Rosings' finest apartments, where the draft did not reach and the morning light warmed the rather sterile space. It was the perfect space to work in, and if she was honest with herself, she rather coveted that apartment. Her own rooms, while warm, thanks to her mother's insistence on her care for her health, were closed off and closeted away so the noise of the household would not disturb her rest. In addition, they were entirely too close to her mother's rooms for her comfort.

Change was a difficult prospect for her mother, so Anne had yet to broach the topic of changing rooms. In time, perhaps, she might be able to make the move. In the meantime, she was content to bide her time until her mother was ready to hear about it.

Still, she hoped Richard would enjoy the space. It was a shame to have it sit empty all the time when it could be in use. Anne liked to imagine Rosings the way she thought her ancestors had meant for it to be when they built it, full of light and laughter, with the sound of children's feet running through the halls.

Anne had never run in the halls. She would never have dared to risk her mother's sharp tongue. But she rather thought her father had in his childhood. Or if not him, then surely this house had once been filled with a happy family.

Sometimes she would walk the gallery in the back hall of the house and wonder about the people in the portraits that lined the walls. Would she have liked them? Would they have smiled at her as a child and applauded her efforts on the pianoforte? Would they have enthused over how beautiful she was as she made her debut in London?

Those were all experiences she would never have. Her mother liked to say she would have been proficient on the pianoforte if she had ever learned, but her mother's concern about her health had kept her from the instrument. Sitting at the pianoforte for hours of practice would have been too taxing. Her nerves could not have handled the mistakes. Excuses abounded.

By the time Anne reached the age when she might have entered society, Lady Catherine had discovered that her importance in Kent far out shadowed any influence she might have in Town. She never even mentioned a possibility of Anne going to London for her debut. Anne secretly thought her mother had realized taking her to London would have meant relinquishing her hold on her. So Anne had resigned herself to Rosings and the life she had there. In time, instead of resenting her entrapment, she had begun to enjoy it and to look for ways to enliven her dreary existence.

She had succeeded. Her contentment here was complete. Still, she had always looked forward to the visit of her cousins and the news they brought of the outside world. Last year had been the most exciting of all, with the arrival of Mrs. Collins, and subsequently Elizabeth Bennet, now Darcy.

Anne had always known she was never bound to become the future Mrs. Darcy, despite what her mother might assert. As soon as she had met Elizabeth Bennet, and saw how her cousin mooned over her, she had known Darcy had found his match. It had just taken her cousin a little longer to come around to the idea.

This year, there was a different sort of excitement at Rosings. Mrs. Collins was expecting a baby, and while that did mean Anne was often deprived of her company around the dinner table, it gave her a wonderful excuse to get out of the house and visit Mrs. Collins at the parsonage, as she had been doing earlier when Richard had come upon her.

Of course, that also meant her mother was taking a keen interest in all the happenings at the parsonage, and she would expect a full report now that Anne had returned.

Anne skirted the main rooms of the house, her mother's strident voice reaching her as she walked the back hallways to her room. She shook her head, a small smile on her face as she imagined Fitzwilliam in the drawing room with her mother, patiently listening as she expounded on one topic or another. The poor, long-suffering man. He really was too good to them. Once inside her chambers, her maid helped her out of her driving clothes and into something her mother would find more suitable for entertaining guests.

Then she was back in the hallways again, heading to the drawing room and her mother. And Richard Fitzwilliam. She must not forget the welcome light he was in the household. That thought had her entering the drawing room with a smile.

Her mother perked up at the sight of her, interrupting her own monologue to say, "Ah! Anne! There you are! Richard told me he ran into you outside the parsonage. How is the dear Mrs. Collins today?"

Anne took her seat on the settee and spared her cousin a glance. "She is as well as can be expected, I suppose. She is rather uncomfortable, but looking forward to the blessed event, which is drawing ever nearer. She will make a fine mother, I am sure."

Lady Catherine harrumphed. "She would be a sight more comfortable if she took to her bed as I advised."

Anne responded, "Mrs. Collins prefers to be active in serving her husband's parishioners, which I applaud. You must admit, Mother, that her presence in the parish would be sorely missed if she were to take to her bed as you suggested."

Her mother waved away her response. "Yes, yes. She is a hard worker, I will grant you that much. It was very well done of Mr. Collins to be so exact in following my instructions when he picked out his wife. He could hardly have found someone else so well suited for the job. I for one quite congratulate myself on a job well done."

Anne resisted the urge to roll her eyes but noticed that Fitzwilliam was not quite as successful. He hid his snort of laughter behind his hand.

Lady Catherine immediately honed in on the sound. "Was that a cough, young man? Are you ill?" She frowned at him.

"You know we cannot have any illness in this household. Anne's health is too precarious."

This time, she could not prevent the eye roll. Thankfully, her mother's full attention was focused on Richard so she did notice. Richard, however, did. His mouth twitched. "I assure you, I am not ill, Aunt Catherine. I simply had something stuck in my throat. I would never jeopardize Anne's health; although I must say that she is looking remarkably well. I would not guess that her health has been a struggle recently."

Anne gave him a smile for his support and the sweet compliment. No one had ever told her she looked remarkably well. No one had ever actually given her a compliment, period. She found it felt nice. Really nice, actually.

Lady Catherine sniffed. "Not recently, per say, but you know she has always had a weak constitution. I do not want her to suffer a relapse when she is finally feeling somewhat well."

Her mother's insistence on her ill health was annoying, especially when she had not been sick in ages, but Anne tried to concentrate on the well-meaning behind her overprotectiveness. She smiled at the room in general. "The sunshine has done wonders for my constitution. I have been greatly enjoying my visits to Mrs. Collins." And with that, the conversation was brought neatly back around to Mrs. Collins.

"I am quite convinced they shall have a son," Lady Catherine said, quickly diving back into one of her favorite topics. "I told Mr. Collins so just the other day. He must have a son. Then I shall be assured that Kent will be left in good hands when he is ready to retire from his post. I told him he must make his sermon this Sunday on the blessings of children and sons in particular. I myself was never granted the gift of a son, but I am quite grateful that I shall have Anne to look after me in my old age. You will never leave me, will you, Anne? It would quite break my heart to have her situated far away from me."

Anne kept her gaze trained on her folded hands and tried not to fidget in her seat. Her mother could spot dissension from a mile away. "You need not worry about that, Mother. I have no plans to marry and move away at the present time." Indeed, she had no such prospects. Her mother had scared away any young man that might have attempted to come calling years ago. Anne was inclined to believe she had done so purposefully, either in a bid to keep her daughter near or to keep the way clear for Darcy.

Lady Catherine nodded. "It is too bad, really. I would so like grandchildren to spoil. Just the idea of having the Collins' little boy running around has made me long for a little one in this house."

Anne and Richard shared an uncomfortable glance. A wistful Lady Catherine was an enigma. Neither he nor she knew quite how to respond.

Then the wistful look on her face twisted into anger. "It is too bad that hussy Elizabeth Bennet stole Darcy away from you. If you had married him and united our two estates, I might have had a grandchild on the way by now. Instead, that silly Mrs. Bennet shall have that honor!"

Anne was rendered speechless by her outburst, but Fitzwilliam was not. He coughed discreetly into his hand. "I believe Mrs. Bennet will have some time to wait for that honor. Regardless, I am sure you would not wish your nephew ill, Aunt Catherine." He smiled his most charming smile, the one that had won him more than one argument in the battlefield of London Society. "I should hate to lose your favor if I should ever marry. You are my favorite aunt after all."

Lady Catherine sniffed. "I am your only living aunt, Richard. Do not try to placate me with clever sayings. It shall not work." Still, she softened. "I am sure that when you do marry you shall make some woman a fine husband. You have never shirked your responsibility to me. Unlike some people we shall not name."

They did not need to be named. Everyone in the room knew who she was talking about. Anne sighed and tried to redirect the conversation to a more productive topic. "Mrs. Collins mentioned that one of the families in the village has been experiencing a leaky roof. I thought it might be wise to have one of the servants go down and see about repairing it. What do you think, Mother?"

Lady Catherine, as always, was eager to share her opinion, and waxed so poetic on the subject that she had still not exhausted the topic by the time they went in to dine.

In fact, she waxed so long and heartily on the subject that she had quite exhausted herself by the time dinner was finished. Anne, sensing Lady Catherine's flagging energy with wisdom born from experience, suggested her mother take herself to bed so that she might be at her best in the morning, when she was to receive Mr. Collins.

Her mother took her advice, leaving Anne and Fitzwilliam to entertain each other in the drawing room. As this was much preferable to allowing Lady Catherine to entertain them, Fitzwilliam did not complain. In fact, he was rather eager to have some time alone with his cousin. She had already surprised him with her beauty, humor, and deft handling of Lady Catherine; he wondered now what other surprises she held in store.

She did not disappoint. As Richard settled into one arm chair, she went to a small desk in the corner of the room and riffled through the contents before pulling out a single sheet of paper.

Paper in hand, she took a seat in the armchair across from his. He watched her curiously, expecting her to share the contents of that note, but instead she simply folded the paper into quarters and laid it on her lap, seemingly content to make him wait.

The inefficiencies of the military should have taught Fitzwilliam patience, but he found that virtue deserting him at the moment. He gestured to the paper she held. "What is that?"

"A list," she answered calmly.

"A list?" he asked.

She nodded.

"Is it for me?"

"I suppose so," she told him.

"What does that mean?" he asked.

She shrugged. "Mother insisted I draw up an accounting of all you and Darcy usually see to while you are here to review the estate. She thought it might be useful to have since this time you shall have to carry Darcy's portion of the work in addition to your own. She did not wish you to forget anything." She glanced at the paper in her hand and added, "I rather thought you also might not wish to forget anything and risk having to return later when my mother discovers it."

Richard could not help chuckling. "You are a wise woman, Anne de Bourgh."

She smiled. "Not wise. Just prepared."

He shook his head. "A rose by any other name…" He held out his hand for the list. "May I see that?"

With a reluctance that confused him, she handed it over. Richard unfolded the sheet, smoothing out the ridges she had created when she folded it, and held it up to the lamp so he could read the writing. It was long and thorough, and Richard was confident that there were items on the list neither he nor Darcy had ever done. Still, he could see the need for every item listed, and found himself determined to see it through to completion. Satisfied, he folded the note back up and slipped it into his pocket for safekeeping.

Anne was eyeing him warily. "So, what do you think, Cousin?"

He smiled at her. "I think it is ambitious, but practical. There is nothing on this list that cannot be done, and nothing that should not be done. It is well-thought out. I shall begin tomorrow morning by going over the books with your steward. That will give me a more complete picture with which to assess the status of the estate."

To his surprise and consternation, she relaxed into her chair, relief passing over her features. He thought the expression a rather strange overreaction to his statement. It was odd that she would have such a strong emotional attachment to that list. How would she have reacted if he had been derogatory?

She did not give him time to dwell on the subject. "Our steward will be happy to have you on hand. He has been singing your praises for weeks. I think it is one of the many factors that motivated my mother to write to you."

Considering that Richard had only had limited interaction with the steward in the past, since that duty mostly fell to Darcy, he found that statement surprising. Richard was an outdoors man, given more to roaming the countryside than going over numbers while he was in Kent. Then again, if the man had been forced to deal with Lady Catherine in the months since he and Darcy had been in Kent, he could well understand the man's anticipation of their return.

Unfortunately, now all of the duties, even the ones he found most onerous, fell on his shoulders since Darcy was no longer welcome at Rosings. He tapped his fingers against his leg in a rapid staccato. "I sincerely doubt he has need of my services. These last few years, the estate has been running in superb condition. It has quite improved."

"I am very pleased to hear you say that." Anne beamed at him, her smile far outweighing the compliment. One might have thought he was complimenting her, not her mother and steward.

His consternation must have shown, for she quickly schooled her features into a more subdued expression. She cleared her throat. "It is always good to know that the estate will go on caring for our needs, especially as Mother has grown older and requires more assistance."

Richard smiled and shook his head. "As long as Mr. Collins is around, I think your mother will be quite content."

Anne laughed, a delightful sound that filled his heart with warmth. How had he lived this long and not known that joy? Laughter was such a precious commodity in this house. He was glad he could be the one to bring out that joy in her.

She rested her head in one palm, turning her warm gaze on him as the firelight flickered over her face, alternately hiding and highlighting her features. "Without Mr. Collins there would be no Mrs. Collins or baby Collins, and so I cannot complain. There has been more life at Rosings since they came than there has been for years."

Her voice turned wistful. "Your visits have always been the only other bright spots." Then she seemed to shake herself out of her melancholy with a wide grin. "We shall see if you can live up to the hype this year without your accomplice. I daresay it will not be as exciting as last year. Tell me, how are Mr. and Mrs. Darcy? Surely, you have heard from them?"

The light in Anne's eyes told him she did not harbor any ill will toward their cousin and his new wife, unlike her mother. She was watching him expectantly, hoping for news. He could not bear to disappoint her. "They are doing well.

Mrs. Darcy is settling in wonderfully at Pemberley. Darcy adores her, Georgiana is emboldened by her, and the staff is captivated. She is a fine mistress. Georgiana will learn much from her."

She smiled broadly. "I am pleased to hear that. I knew she and Darcy were well-matched. It was only a matter of time before they realized it for themselves. He is so very different when he is comfortable among family."

Richard nodded. "The effect is only enhanced now that he is married. He is fortunate she learned his true personality before he scared her off forever. He had not endeared himself to her when they were here last."

"No, but it was the beginning of a turning point. They needed only time and opportunity for their love to grow." That assessing gaze, which had so easily seen past Darcy's foibles, turned on him. "And how about you, Richard? What news do you have?"

He was not as comfortable now that her focus was on him. "I have sold my commission, as you may be aware."

She nodded. "Yes. Your mother wrote mine when word of that reached her. She was very surprised."

He sighed. "She very well may have been. I was surprised."

That statement prompted her to cock her head and look at him questioningly. "What brought about the change?"

He shrugged. "It was not a life I wanted anymore. There was too much worry and responsibility. I could not bear the thought of going to war again. After a while, I found taking orders to be burdensome and I no longer needed the prominence to feel secure in my position. It was time to let it go and seek other avenues. I do not have the wealth Darcy does, nor will I ever, but my future is secure between my family's holdings and my own."

She nodded, commenting sagely, "Contentment is a fine quality, Richard, and one I have found most helpful. Wealth does not equate happiness, as we both well know."

He could only agree with her. "It is the truth."

She shifted in her seat. "How did your parents handle the news?"

A corner of his mouth turned up. "My mother found it necessary to write to her sister, did she not? I think they were shocked, but have been supportive for the most part. I think Mother is relieved to no longer be constantly worried about my safety."

"I think that was a relief for the entire family," Anne admitted. "I know I rejoiced when I heard the news." A smile spread across her face. "I was also very pleased to know I would not have to be the one to audit the books this year."

Richard chuckled. "I very much doubt your mother would ever ask you to do that."

She snorted, in a very unladylike fashion that Richard found surprisingly delightful. "Ask? No. Demand? Perhaps."

The clock in the hall struck the hour and they both started in surprise at the time. Anne rose in a swirl of skirts. "Forgive me, Cousin. I had no idea how late it had grown. You have traveled a long way today. I must not keep you from your rest."

Richard stood, strangely loath to leave, even though his body had begun to protest the lateness of the hour some time ago. "Do not blame yourself, Anne. I have had a wonderful time catching up with you. I only regret that your steward will keep me very busy in the days to come. We shall have very little time to spend together."

A corner of her mouth turned up. "Not too busy for a little light-hearted entertainment, I hope. Mother has requested that you join us for a dinner party she is hosting later in the week."

"I shall look forward to it." He bowed over her hand. "Mayhap the books will be in good order and I shall see more of you than I expect."

She smiled genially. "One can hope." She curtseyed and turned to go up to her room. "Good night, Cousin."

Richard watched her go, although he was the one who should have claimed fatigue long ago and retired. His valet was surely waiting up for him. Yet, he could not bring himself to abandon the room where Anne had come to life.

Rosings was not precisely the hostile environment he had always thought it to be. Even his rooms this time around were warm and inviting, and he could not help but wonder if his cousin had been the source of that welcome surprise as well.

From everything he was learning about her, it seemed to fit. Certainly, he had never felt so at home within the walls of Rosings; no, nor in the whole of Kent. His ready good nature usually stood him in good stead here, along with a healthy dose of the outdoors, but he wondered if another tactic might not be even more useful for his sanity. Or rather, another person.

He had told Anne he was unlikely to see much of her while he was here, but he heartily hoped that it did not turn out to be the case. If he had anything to do with it, it would not. While he normally dreaded Aunt Catherine's dinner parties, he found himself looking forward to the opportunity to be with Anne again.

Sometimes, change was good.

The prospect alive in his mind, he went upstairs to find his bed, whistling jauntily.

Other books by Lelia M. Silver

The story of Pride and Prejudice continues with…
The Children of Pride and Prejudice series

Emilia's Folly

John's Downfall

Sophia's Champion

Thea's Legacy

Helene's Honor

Hannah's Viscount

Theo's Choice

Eliza's Journey

Pride and Prejudice goes for a spin in the Old West with…
Pemberley Creek series

Pride and Presumption

Pride and Perfection

A modern twist to Pride and Prejudice

Pride and Precipice

Fall in love with small-town life in Oakham, Ohio with...

Oakham Hearts series

Hearts with History

Hearts with Hope

Hearts Alight

To find out more visit:
https://www.leliamsilver.com